"The Bluford Series is mind-blowing!"
— *Adam A.*

"These books are *deep*. They show readers who are going through difficult problems that they are not alone in the world. And they even help teach you how to deal with situations in a positive way."
— *Vianny C.*

"I love all of the books in the Bluford Series. They are page-turners full of secrets, surprises, and lots of drama."
— *Kayli A.*

"Each Bluford book starts out with a bang. And then, when you turn the page, it gets even better!"
— *Alex M.*

"The Bluford Series is amazing! They make you feel like you're inside the story, like everything's happening to you."
— *Ricardo N.*

"These are life-changing stories that make you think long after you read the last page."

"I found it very ____ these books. They ____ beginning to end a ____ The characters are vivid, and the ____ me in eager anticipation of the next book."
— *Keziah J.*

ADELANTE

"For the first time in high school, I read a book I liked. For real, the Bluford Series is *tight*."

—Jermaine B.

"These are thrilling, suspenseful books filled with real-life scenarios that make them too good to put down."

—DeAndria B.

"My school is just like Bluford High. The characters are just like people I know. These books are *real!*"

—Jessica K.

"I have never been so interested in books in my entire life. I'm surprised how much the Bluford Series catches my attention. Once I start reading, I can't stop. I keep staying up into the midnight hours trying to finish."

— Andrew C.

"The Bluford Series are the best books I have ever read. They are like TVs in my head."

— Yaovi C.

"One of my friends told me how good the Bluford Series is. She was right. Once I started reading, I couldn't stop, not even to sleep!"

— Bibi R.

"I love the Bluford books and the stories they tell. They're so real and action-packed, I feel like I'm inside the pages, standing next to the characters!"

—Michael D.

Promises to Keep

Paul Langan

Series Editor: Paul Langan

TOWNSEND PRESS
www.townsendpress.com

Books in the Bluford Series

Copyright © 2013 by Townsend Press, Inc.
Printed in the United States of America

9 8 7 6 5 4 3

Cover illustration © 2013 by Gerald Purnell

Townsend Press, Inc.
439 Kelley Drive
West Berlin, NJ 08091
permissions@townsendpress.com

ISBN: 978-1-59194-303-7

Library of Congress Control Number:
2012953523

Chapter 1

"C'mon, wake up."

Tyray Hobbs opened his eyes and glanced at his clock. It was 5:03 a.m. He had been asleep for only a few hours.

Was yesterday just a bad dream? he wondered.

"I said WAKE UP!" ordered Gil Hobbs, Tyray's father. He was standing in the bedroom doorway, already dressed in jeans and work boots, the same ones he wore every day on the job as a construction foreman.

"What for? It's early," Tyray replied. "School ain't startin' for hours."

"We ain't goin' to Bluford. You and me got something else to do first," his father barked.

Tyray sat up and squinted at the

1

hallway light that shined into his room. After what happened last night, he didn't want to get up or think about anything.

"Where we goin'?"

"We gotta get that gun you left in the alley," Dad answered soberly. "We can't leave it where some kids might pick it up. It's probably got your fingerprints all over it, too," he grumbled. "Don't need no cops haulin' you away. One son is bad enough."

Tyray winced at his father's words. He knew Dad was talking about Warren, his older brother, who had been dragged out of their house by the police over a year ago. He was arrested for armed robbery. Since then, Dad had become a bitter, quick-tempered man who yelled more than anything. Tyray knew he had given his father many reasons to yell, especially last night.

"C'mon. *Move*," Dad ordered. "We gotta go."

Tyray stumbled to the bathroom and shut the door. He froze at his reflection in the mirror. His eyes were puffy and bloodshot. The cast that encased his left hand was stained with droplets of mud. A painful scab stretched just under his hairline. He looked terrible. The events of last night flooded through his mind like scenes from a nightmare.

The cold heaviness of the gun in his hand.

The terror in Darrell Mercer's eyes as Tyray's finger slid over the trigger.

The final moment when, instead of at Darrell, he had pointed the gun at himself.

Tyray shuddered. He turned on the water and splashed his face, trying to drive away the memories. Fifteen years old and nearly six feet tall, Tyray had spent his days as a freshman at Bluford High School tormenting Darrell, a new kid from Philadelphia. He had robbed him of his lunch money, tripped him in gym class, tossed him in a trash can at a school dance, and sent him home in tears more than once. But then one day, during lunch period two weeks ago, Darrell stood up to him.

"You ain't nothing but a bully," he had said.

At first, Tyray didn't know what to do. None of the kids he had hassled since middle school ever challenged him. Broad and muscular for his age, Tyray had kept them too scared to do that, let alone snitch to a teacher.

But Darrell was different. He had joined Bluford's wrestling team and had gradually become more popular at school. And when he spoke up in front of everyone, he said something else, words that stung each time Tyray remembered them.

"No one in this school likes you. They're just scared of you. But you know what? I ain't afraid of you no more."

People whooped at the insult. Others rushed forward like hungry dogs that smelled blood.

"Fight, fight, fight!" some yelled. A crowd quickly formed. It seemed everyone in the cafeteria was eager to see what would happen next.

Tyray snapped. Every cell in his body was ready to destroy Darrell right there. He didn't care if he got suspended. Losing his reputation was far worse. But when he swung his fists at the smaller boy, it all went wrong.

Darrell was quick. He dodged Tyray's punches. Then, in a flash, he used a wrestling move, lifting Tyray up and slamming him down on the rock-hard cafeteria floor. When Tyray landed, his left wrist snapped like a tree branch. He screamed in pain

4

clutching his hand. Some in the crowd nodded and smirked at him. A few even laughed.

Principal Spencer gave Tyray a three-day suspension for fighting. Afterward he became a joke at school. People who used to join him in teasing Darrell now laughed at him. Others, including his old friend Rodney Banks, acted as if he didn't exist. That's when Tyray decided he needed a gun.

"C'mon, boy!" Dad yelled from out in the hallway. "We ain't got all day."

"I'll be out in a minute!" Tyray hollered, quickly washing himself and rushing to his room to throw on some jeans and a black hoodie.

Minutes later, Tyray sat in his father's noisy pickup, gazing out at Union Street. In the dreary gray dawn, the normally busy avenue looked deserted. Apartment windows were dark. Storefronts stood shuttered and empty. Some were hidden behind thick steel mesh that made them look like jails.

"This neighborhood's goin' down-hill," his father mumbled as he drove.

Outside, the familiar buildings passed by in a dull blur. The Laundromat. Metro Cell Phones. Wilson's Pharmacy. Quick

5

Check-Cashing. The pawnshop with the ugly "Cash 4 Gold" sign. Further up the block, closer to Bluford, was Graham's store and then Phat Burger, the fast food joint where Tyray hung out many times after school, usually with money he stole from Darrell. It all seemed so long ago.

"Gonna be like 43rd Street around here soon. You'll see," Dad grumbled.

Tyray cringed. He knew all about 43rd Street. It was the first place he went to buy a gun. He had gone straight to Jupiter James, a Bluford dropout everyone knew was a drug dealer. Jupiter's older brother, Londell, would have been Tyray's first choice, but he was locked up last year for attempted murder.

The night Tyray went to pick up the weapon, he got jumped. Someone smashed his head with a stick and robbed him while he was down. Tyray was so desperate afterward that he stole money from Mom. He used it to buy a gun from Bones, a scary old thug who had been in the neighborhood for years. Bones sold him the weapon right behind Phat Burger.

Tyray's hand trembled slightly as he spotted the side street where he had met Bones. He buried it in his sleeve so Dad wouldn't see. A minute later they arrived at the store where Darrell worked. Tyray's stomach sank.

"It's back there," he said, pointing to an alley that ran along the edge of the store parking lot. The asphalt was slick from rain that had fallen the night before. A few sections were cracked and sunken, making shallow puddles the size of graves.

Dad's jaws were clenched. A vein bulged just behind his temple as he wheeled the pickup around and pulled to a stop. He shoved the gear into park and yanked the keys from the ignition.

"Show me," he grunted.

Tyray felt an acid taste in his mouth as he led his father to the straggly shrubs where he had hidden the night before, waiting for Darrell.

"Here," he said, feeling as if he were about to vomit. "I was . . . we were here." He pointed to where he had knocked Darrell off his bike. A muddy gash marked where the bicycle tires had scraped the ground. Just hours earlier he had stood in the same spot, pointing a gun at Darrell's head. The moment flashed through his mind.

"Please don't kill me," Darrell had

7

cried, tears running down his face, his voice cracked and choked with fear. In the gloomy drizzle, Darrell had looked like a child, not a fifteen-year-old. *"Please!"* he had begged.

All Tyray had to do was pull the trigger, and Darrell Mercer would have been gone. Erased.

But Tyray couldn't do it.

He had never wanted to be a killer, but somehow things had gotten out of control. A near failure at school, Tyray had been almost friendless since Darrell humiliated him. He couldn't imagine going back to school with everyone hating him. He could see only one way out, one way to make it all go away. He raised the gun away from Darrell and pointed it at his own skull. His hand trembled in the quiet drizzle, and he braced for the blast he knew was coming.

BOOM!

But just before he had pulled the trigger, Darrell dove at him, knocking his hand away. The shot thundered harmlessly into the air. If Darrell had been a second slower, Tyray knew he never would have made it home.

His parents looked stunned when he crept in three hours late, covered in

8

mud, his eyes wet from rain and sweat and tears. Mr. Mitchell, his English teacher, was there. He had heard the rumors in school that Tyray had a gun, and he came to talk to his parents. Facing them, Tyray confessed his problems at Bluford and how he had bought a gun. But he never told them about putting the gun to his own head.

"I didn't do nothin' to Darrell," he explained. *"I knew it wasn't right, so I just threw the gun away. That's all that happened. I swear."*

Mr. Mitchell nodded grimly as Tyray spoke. Later, Tyray overheard the teacher suggest they see a family counselor. Dad shrugged off the idea.

"I respect what you're sayin', Mr. Mitchell, but we can handle our own problems. We don't need someone comin' in here tellin' us how to raise our son."

Tyray was relieved. He didn't want some stranger trying to figure out what he had almost done. But he could tell by his mother's eyes that she disagreed with Dad's decision, though she didn't say anything. It was always that way.

"Where is it?" Dad asked, breaking his thoughts. He was hunched over a thick clump of weeds looking for the weapon. "Which way did you throw it?"

Tyray studied the ground and retraced his steps. He walked over to where he stood when Darrell shoved his arm. Nearby was a muddy puddle the size of a headstone. Tyray peered into the shallow black pool.

He could see the gun, its barrel barely peeking up from the murky water. It was pointed right at his feet.

"It's right here—"

"Don't touch it!" Dad snapped, darting in front of him. He reached into the puddle and pulled out the weapon. Its slick metal glistened weakly in the dim morning light.

"C'mon, let's go," Dad huffed, throwing it into a white plastic bag and rushing back to the truck as if he were afraid others might see them. Seconds later, they were heading home.

"I still can't believe what you did!" Dad barked. He gunned the accelerator and the old truck lurched forward.

Tyray said nothing. He kept his eyes locked on the streets outside his window. Anything to avoid his father's face.

"This ain't over yet, neither," Dad fumed. "What if his family presses charges?"

"Darrell wouldn't do that. He ain't no snitch. He never told anyone the whole time I was hassling him," Tyray admitted.

"Oh, so you got it all figured out now, is that what you're sayin'?" Dad asked, smacking the steering wheel as they pulled to a stop at an intersection. Across from them, a police car waited at a red light. Dad eyed it nervously. "You think his momma's gonna sit still when he tells her some boy from school put a gun to his head?"

Tyray rubbed his forehead. He hadn't thought of that. Would Darrell tell her what happened?

"Cops might come for you yet, and I won't be able to do nothin' about it," Dad said as the light turned green. They both watched in silence as the police car slowly passed. Tyray glanced in the rear-view mirror to see the car stop, turn around and begin following them.

Maybe I shoulda never come home, Tyray thought. *Maybe I woulda been better off if Darrell were slower. Just a second or two.*

The dark thoughts swirled in his mind as they returned to their small rancher. The police car trailed them the entire way back. Finally, as they pulled into the driveway, it passed by.

Dad sighed, wiped his brow, and grabbed the plastic bag with the gun.

"So where'd you get this thing, any-way?"

Tyray shrugged. He wasn't sure how to answer.

"Boy, I'm talkin' to you! Look at me. Where'd you get this gun?" Dad repeated.

Tyray glanced up at his father. Deep creases lined his forehead, and a vein throbbed in his neck. His left hand still clutched the steering wheel.

"Don't make me repeat myself again," Dad warned.

Tyray didn't know what to do. If he didn't answer, Dad might hit him. He could see it in his eyes. It was as if his father had forgotten the promises he had made to Mr. Mitchell last night.

"I'm gonna try and be more patient with him," he had said when he shook the teacher's hand.

"Speak, boy!" Dad boomed, grabbing the collar of Tyray's sweatshirt in his fist.

"*Bones*," Tyray wanted to say. He pic-tured the skinny man with the voice that crackled like dry leaves and a cough that

12

sounded like death itself. *"I got it from some scary dude named Bones."*

But Tyray couldn't say the name. He was afraid that if word got out, Bones might come after him or his family. He had heard stories in the neighborhood and knew the man was dangerous. Bones even admitted to him that he had killed someone.

"Some dude on 43rd Street. I never seen him before," Tyray lied. "I don't even know his name. I just gave him the money and that was it."

His father shoved him back against the passenger door as if Tyray's words disgusted him.

"Don't be lying to me, Tyray. Not after all this. If you're protectin' one of your friends—"

"I ain't lyin', Dad. I swear." Tyray tried his best to sound convincing, but he could see his father wasn't fooled. He had gone to 43rd Street to buy a gun from Londell James, but he ended up getting robbed by some kids instead. That's when he turned to Bones.

"Boy, I don't even want to look at you right now," Dad fumed. He took his keys and the plastic bag and stormed toward the house.

"What's wrong?" Mom said, meeting Dad at the door.

"He's lying. Right now, after everything that happened, he's *still* lying. I don't care what Mr. Mitchell says," Dad growled, turning and pointing at him. "He don't know you like I do. Your butt is grounded. Y'hear me?"

Tyray shrugged. *"If I'da been faster, you wouldn't have to bother with me no more, Dad. Maybe then you'd be happy,"* he wanted to say, but his mouth felt glued shut. He couldn't speak.

"I don't even want to look at his lyin' face right now!" Dad yelled.

"Gil, please."

"What? He coulda killed a boy last night!" his father hollered, slamming his fist against the side of the house.

"But he *didn't*," Mom insisted, touching his shoulders. "He walked away. He knew better."

"Yeah, well how come he didn't know better when he stole your money? Or when he snuck out in the middle of the night and hid a gun in his mattress? Or when he was beatin' up that boy for months? Or when he lied to my face just now? Huh?" Dad barked, hurling questions like punches.

14

Mom stepped back, as if Dad's words hurt.

"I'll tell you why. 'Cause he's no good!" Dad yelled, shouldering past her into the house, carrying the plastic bag. "He's gonna throw his life away too, just like his brother."

"Gil, you know that's not true," Mom protested, but Dad was already inside.

Tyray heard a door slam and something shatter in the kitchen. He flinched at the sound and sat down on the front stoop. For years, he mostly ignored Dad's rants, which had become much worse since Warren was arrested. But this time was different. This time, Dad's words cut like a dagger in his heart.

Tyray knew his father was right.

Chapter 2

"He's no good!"

Tyray still heard Dad's voice in his head as he forced himself to Bluford High School and darted toward the back row of his English class.

Thunk!

Tyray's cast bumped someone's desk, sending a book slapping to the floor. He ignored it and tried to pretend everything was normal. But as he neared his seat, he could feel his classmates watching him. Mr. Mitchell and Darrell hadn't yet arrived.

Maybe Darrell's snitching on me right now, Tyray thought. He imagined the smaller boy talking to Principal Spencer. If so, he knew he would be called to the office and have to admit to everyone what really happened. The idea made his stomach churn.

Tyray glanced around the notice-ably quiet classroom. The stares of his classmates seemed to crawl all over him. He knew they had heard the rumors that he had a gun. But had they heard worse? Did Darrell tell them the truth? Is that why they were watching him? Tyray couldn't stand it.

"Whatchu all lookin' at?" he grum-bled finally.

No one answered.

Jamee Wills and Amberlynn Bailey, two girls on the cheerleading squad, turned away as if he were beneath them. Rodney Banks, his old friend, shrugged his shoulders and ignored him. Tasha Jenkins whispered some-thing to Janelle Wiggins, and they both shook their heads. Other students flipped through notebooks and acted as if he wasn't even there.

Only Harold Davis, Darrell's best friend, faced him. Normally, Harold was too scared to even look his way. But now the chubby boy eyed him warily. Had Darrell called Harold last night and told him everything?

You shoulda seen him, Harold. He was sittin' in this puddle cryin' like a

17

baby. For real, I couldn't believe it," Tyray imagined Darrell saying. It made him cringe.

Harold rose from his desk and walked toward him. Tyray suddenly felt cornered. He couldn't just sit there and wait for what was coming.

"Whatchu want, fat boy?" Tyray challenged, standing up. "Ain't you got a sandwich to eat or something?" He had teased Harold countless times about his weight, calling him Heavy-D or HD back when they were in middle school. But now he didn't want to insult Harold. He just wanted him and everyone else to go away.

Harold shrugged and lowered his eyes to the ground.

"Nah," he mumbled. "I just want my book."

Tyray followed Harold's eyes and saw a book lying at his feet, a worn copy of their latest English reading assignment, *Lord of the Flies.* Tyray realized he had knocked it to the floor when he rushed into the classroom.

Careful to hide his relief, Tyray sucked his teeth and kicked the book toward the large boy. Harold crouched over, grunted, and grabbed it.

"Man you better stop eatin', Heavy-D," Tyray teased, trying to pretend everything was the same as always, "or you're gonna need a bra."

"Why you gotta be so rude?" said a voice from the other side of the room. Tyray looked over to see Jamee Wills. "At least Harold don't go stealing money from girls."

Tyray winced. He didn't need Jamee to remind him of what he had done to Lark Collins. The shy, frumpy girl was the only person who had been nice to him after his humiliation in the cafeteria. But Tyray had used her, convincing her to give him forty dollars for a gift for his mother. He actually wanted the money to buy a gun. When Lark found out that he had lied to her, she flashed him a sad look that tore his insides with guilt. Tyray pictured it when he held the gun to his head.

"Ain't no one said your name, Jamee. Why don't you just mind your own business," he snapped.

The classroom was filling. Tyray knew everyone was listening. He wished Jamee would just shut up and leave him alone.

"My friend *is* my business," Jamee huffed. "Maybe you'd understand if you

19

had some friends."

A few students gasped at her words. Tasha pulled out her cell phone and texted something, her thumbs working in a feverish blur.

Tyray tried to pretend Jamee's comment meant nothing, but for an instant he was speechless. Part of him felt the urge to slap the smug look right off her face, the way Dad sometimes treated him. But he could never hit a girl.

"Jamee, if my friends were anything like you, I'd rather be alone," he grumbled, trying to act as if nothing had changed, as if the moment in the alley didn't haunt him, as if his father's words weren't eating invisibly at his chest.

"I don't know why Lark ever talked to you," Jamee said, turning away from him. "She's too good for you."

Tyray cursed under his breath and slouched in his seat. He knew she was right.

Just then, Darrell Mercer stepped into the class. An ugly scrape covered his right elbow. Tyray knew it was from when he had knocked him off his bike. For an instant, Tyray pictured him lifeless at his feet. It had all come so close.

Darrell sat down and glanced back

once at Tyray. "Wassup," he said quickly before turning around and facing the front of the room.

Tyray froze, unable to speak. His throat felt as if someone was gripping his neck. The entire classroom hushed. It was as if everyone was stunned by Darrell's gesture. Even Harold, Darrell's close friend, looked puzzled.

Did you see that? Ain't they supposed to be hatin' on each other? Tyray could see the questions on their faces. Their surprise told him Darrell had kept quiet. He hadn't told them what happened. Not yet.

RING!

The first period bell blasted overhead. Mr. Mitchell walked in, shattering the moment. He glanced for a half second at Tyray and began taking attendance as he did every other school day. It was as if yesterday had never happened.

"Today we're going to talk about violence," Mr. Mitchell said then, picking up his copy of *Lord of the Flies*. "We've all seen it. Too many of us have experienced it, including some of you. Me too," he added with a look toward Darrell. "I want to know why."

A few students grumbled and rolled their eyes. Others shrugged as if what he said made no sense. But most turned to the front of the room. Tyray was relieved to finally escape their stares.

"I'm serious. How can we stop what we don't understand? We lose more young people in this country to shootings each year than we do in wars. I am tired of it. I don't want to lose anyone else, especially not you, so let's explore this problem," Mr. Mitchell continued.

"Many folks have theories about violence. Some blame society. They say people are born peaceful but that civilization—money and power—makes them violent. Others say people are born violent and that civilization—laws and police—keep us safe."

A few students snickered at the mention of the police, but Mr. Mitchell ignored them. "Your book talks about this. But before we get started, I wonder what *you* think. Where does violence come from?"

Tyray squirmed in his seat. He didn't want to hear about violence or the police, especially after last night. The images of what had almost happened blazed raw and fresh in his mind. He felt like getting up and walking out of the classroom. Instead, he slouched low at his desk and waited for class to end. The teacher didn't call on him the entire period.

"Can I speak with you, Tyray?" Mr. Mitchell asked as soon as class ended.

Tyray nodded. After last night, he expected it.

"Listen," Mr. Mitchell began, careful to shut the door once the class emptied.

Tyray braced himself. He knew some students liked Mr. Mitchell because he tried to help them with their problems. Until yesterday, Tyray thought the teacher was nosey.

"I know things have been rough on you, but I want to tell you something. No matter what anyone says or what you're feeling inside, you need to know what you did last night was brave."

"Brave?"

Tyray couldn't look the teacher in the eye. Normally, he would say Mr. Mitchell's words were corny and stupid. Now Tyray thought he was just plain wrong. *"You don't understand. You don't even know what happened,"* he wanted to say.

"That's right. You were brave enough to walk away. Not everyone does that,

Tyray. They're so worried about their reputation that they do something they know is wrong. Or worse, some of them are so hurt inside they don't care anymore. Not you. I can see you care. You faced all that stuff down and did the right thing. That's what being a man is."

But you don't know what I was about to do, Tyray thought. *You don't know nothin'*. Tyray's words caught in his throat.

"And because you did that, Darrell's still here, and you're still here, and no one's in jail," Mr. Mitchell explained. "And no one's mother is crying this morning. It could've been very different. We both know that."

Tyray stared at the floor. His eyes started to burn and sting.

"You changed your whole life just like that." Mr. Mitchell snapped his fingers to make his point. "There's a whole world out there, Tyray. Bigger than this school or someone's reputation. Because you walked away, you still got a chance to see it. I'm happy you made the choice you did. So's your dad, even though he might not know how to show it."

Tyray cringed at the mention of Dad.

"He ain't happy about nothin'," Tyray

grumbled. *"Especially me."*

Mr. Mitchell nodded. "Look, if you ever need to talk, I know someone who—"

"Need to talk?" Tyray repeated. "Man, whatchu tryin' to say?"

"C'mon, Tyray. We both know you have a lot going on. Sometimes it can help to sit down with someone. I know a counselor. He's helped a lot of young people, and I think he could help you."

"I don't need no counselor or whatever. There ain't nothin' wrong with me," he said, rising from his seat, angry with himself for almost letting the teacher get to him. There was no way he was going to tell some stranger what almost happened. No way.

"Tyray—"

"Sorry, but I gotta go, Mr. Mitchell. I don't wanna be late," he said, storming off to his next class.

"How we doing, Mr. Hobbs?" Principal Spencer asked Tyray hours later. She stood in her usual spot at the cafeteria doorway, eyeing students as they approached for lunch.

"I'm fine, Ms. Spencer," Tyray grumbled. He slipped his brother's old iPod deep in the pocket of his black hoodie so she wouldn't see it.

"Things a little better today?" she asked, peering at him curiously. He knew she had heard the rumors too. She even had his locker searched for a gun earlier in the week. Of course, she found nothing. He had kept the weapon away from school.

No, Ms. Spencer, they ain't no better. But whatchu gonna do about it? he wanted to say. Instead he nodded.

"Yeah, they great. Never better," he said.

"I hope so," she said with an edge to her voice.

He barged past her into the noisy cafeteria. The air was filled with the roar of students talking, the slap of backpacks hitting the ground, the groan of plastic chairs scraping against the tile floor.

Tyray glanced at the spot where his whole world had crashed down just two weeks ago. He knew the cafeteria was full of people who had witnessed it and laughed at him, people who had pretended to like him until that day.

"I never liked you, neither," he mumbled to himself, fighting back the anger that still boiled in his chest.

He grabbed the iPod from his pocket

and stepped into the lunch line when a familiar face came through the side door. It was Lark. Wearing loose jeans and a frumpy purple sweatshirt, she stepped to her table and dropped her heavy denim book bag.

Back in middle school, he used to chuckle when girls like Natalie Wallace and Shanetta Greene teased Lark for being quiet and always having her nose stuck in a book. He had even laughed along, but Lark never held it against him. When he broke his wrist, she didn't join others in teasing him. Instead, she told him she felt bad about what had happened.

And all I did was take her money, he thought.

"C'mon, man! Stop daydreaming. Move!"

The voice shattered Tyray's thoughts. He turned around and realized the line had moved forward. He was holding everyone up.

"Wake up, yo!" someone else yelled. "I'm hungry."

Tyray cursed and stepped forward. He had stolen money from lots of kids, including Darrell, never thinking twice about it. But something about Lark

27

made him feel worse than all the others. Maybe it was the innocent way she smiled at him, as if she saw something in him no one else could see.

He cranked up the iPod to block out his thoughts and grabbed a tray of spongy chicken nuggets and watery green beans.

Some say to be great
Is to be misunderstood.
But they don't come to
My neighborhood.

He swaggered out with his food, letting the music drown out the voices of everyone around him. But then he saw her again. Lark. Now Jamee, Cindy, and Amberlynn had joined her at the table.

"She's too good for you," Jamee had said. He knew she was right. If only he could pay Lark back.

Where school is a prison
And a prison is a school
And livin' is passin'
And survivin' is the rule.

The music pounded as each girl at Lark's table turned and glared at him. If only he could show Lark he was sorry, that he had thought of her the moment he had raised the gun to his head. But how? He had no money.

Do you feel me?
Can you even hear?
I'ma scream louder
Before I disappear.

And then it hit him. He yanked off his earphones and walked toward their table. Why hadn't he thought of it before? It would only take a minute.

"Hey, wassup, Lark?" he said, ignoring the stares that locked on him like gun sights.

"Will you just leave her alone?" Jamee said before Lark could even respond. "She's over you. Done. See ya!"

"Yeah, she don't want nothin' to do with you," Amberlynn added.

"I ain't talking to neither of you!" Tyray shot back. All he needed was a minute with Lark. That's all it would take. "Lark, can we talk?"

"What do you want?" asked Lark finally. He could see the tiny hairline scar above her lip. She had told him she'd gotten it when she fell down her grandma's steps when she was a kid. Tyray wasn't sure if that was the truth.

29

"You don't need to talk to him, Lark," cut in Jamee. "Ignore him. He's just a wannabe thug who got what he deserves."

Jamee's words hit Tyray like a slap in the face.

"Girl, I'm sick of all y'all talkin' 'bout me!" he snapped, unable to control himself. "You don't know nothin'! Why don't you just keep your ugly mug outta my business?"

Heads turned toward them. Tyray could feel it all slipping out of control. Like always. He noticed that his voice sounded like Dad's.

"Why? Whatchu gonna do? Shoot her with your cast?" mocked Donté, a sophomore from a nearby table. All his friends erupted in laughter.

"Yeah, he gonna be like this," joked Luiz, one of Darrell's friends from the wrestling team. As he spoke, he crumpled up his sleeve into a mock broken arm and then pretended to shoot it as if it were a pathetic gun.

The laughter spread like wildfire. Tyray gripped his tray, fighting the urge to swing it at Luiz's face.

"I told you," Donté said. "He all talk. Been dishin' it out all year, but now he can't take it."

"Yo, c'mon guys," a voice cut in. "Just drop it, all right?"

He turned to see Darrell stepping toward them, carrying his lunch. Tyray's stomach sank. It was bad enough that he had seen him cry. Now the smaller boy was standing up for him. It was almost more humiliating than when he had broken his wrist. He wanted Darrell to shut up, but he couldn't bring himself to say it, not after what happened.

The cafeteria suddenly felt as if it was closing in. The stares. The laughter. The whispers. Darrell's pity. Tyray had to get out.

Without a word, he slammed his tray on an empty table. Silverware clanged to the floor. Food splattered. Hundreds of heads spun around to see what was happening. Tyray grabbed his brother's old iPod.

"Here," he said tensely, putting it down in front of Lark.

It was the only thing he had that was worth any money, his one chance to do something right, no matter what everyone else thought. He needed her to have it.

"What's this?" she asked.

"I owe you forty dollars. I wanted to

31

pay you back, and this is all I got right now," he explained.

Jamee and Amberlynn looked up at him as if he had just spoken a strange language. Lark stood up.

"Tyray, I can't keep this," she said.

But he ignored her. He stepped over the mess and headed toward the door.

"Tyray?" Lark called. "Tyray?!"

He stormed out, not once looking back.

Chapter 3

"You all right?" Darrell Mercer asked.

They were in gym class, waiting for Mr. Dooling to take attendance. Tyray hadn't said a word to Darrell since the blowup in the cafeteria last week. The episode only seemed to make Tyray the target of even more jokes at school.

"Why you talkin' to me?" Tyray asked. Each time he saw Darrell's face, the scene in the alley replayed in his mind.

"Well, after everything . . ." Darrell stammered. "With the guys in the cafeteria and all . . . I just thought—"

"Look, just 'cause all that happened don't mean we're friends. We both know that ain't true. You don't gotta pretend," Tyray said, glancing at his cast. "Besides, the whole school's gonna think I'm a punk if you stick up for me again."

"Who cares what they think?"

"Like you even understand," Tyray grumbled.

"Are you serious?" Darrell said. "After what you did to me all year?"

"Oh, so that's what this is about? You tryin' to rub it in my face?"

"No, I'm just sayin'—"

"Or maybe you feelin' sorry for me after what you saw . . ." Tyray said, a wave of bitterness sweeping over him. "I don't need you or anyone lookin' down on me."

"It's not like that! Man, you gotta stop—"

"Stop what? You don't even know what's going on, Mercer, so don't tell me what I gotta do," Tyray fumed. "Pretend what you saw never happened. Go hang with Harold or your little wrestling crew. I don't need no one watchin' my back, especially not you. Y'hear me?"

"Quiet back there!" Mr. Dooling yelled from the front of the gym.

"Yeah, Mr. Dooling. Tell this boy to be quiet," Tyray said. It took all his effort to hide the emotion in his voice, a mix of anger, hurt, and shame.

Darrell shook his head and turned away.

Tyray avoided him for the rest of the period, sitting on the bleachers with his broken wrist while everyone else ran laps on the track behind the high school. When class finally ended, Tyray rushed straight to his locker. He was dialing his combination when he spotted Lark at the end of the hallway. She was coming toward him.

He pretended he didn't notice, hoping he could sneak out without having to face her. He yanked open his locker, grabbed his jacket, and slammed it shut. He was ready to dash down the hallway when she called out.

"Tyray, wait!"

He took a step but then stopped himself, fighting the urge to walk away and leave her there in the hallway. She was at his side in seconds, though he could barely stand to look at her. Shame and guilt pulled his eyes away from hers.

"What do you want?" he asked.

"I didn't mean for that to happen. I'm sorry."

"For what?" He avoided her eyes. He didn't want her sympathy. It only made him feel worse.

"Everybody in the cafeteria the other

35

day. They shouldn'ta said those things to you."

Tyray shrugged. "Why not? Maybe they're right," he mumbled. "Look, I ain't got time to talk right now. I'm grounded and my dad is gonna flip out if I'm late."

A crowd of students passed by and Lark stepped closer to him. "Here," she said, holding out the iPod. "Take this."

"Nah, it's yours." He refused to take it and turned to walk away, but Lark grabbed his arm. The sleeve of his sweatshirt pulled back, revealing the bone-like cast. She gasped in surprise and let go awkwardly.

"I'm sorry, Tyray. But I can't keep it. It belongs to you. When you get the money, you can pay me back then."

"Girl, please. Just let me do this," he said, annoyed at how desperate he sounded. He needed to repay her somehow, to prove to himself he could do something right, at least to her. Just one thing, no matter what his father or anyone else said.

"I never shoulda lied to you and taken your money," he added, remembering the way Lark had looked at him.

He could feel her staring at him, but

the shame he felt kept his eyes locked on the floor. All he could see was Lark's heavy book bag. It was covered in tiny tan hairs. She seemed to notice and started brushing them off.

"My cat," she said as if she were slightly embarrassed. "She's shedding. You like cats?" she asked, as if she was trying to change the subject.

"They all right, I guess," he replied. For years, he had wanted to have a pet, but Dad always said no.

"We have two of them. You can borrow Ginger if you want. She's the one who's shedding. Your cast might look good covered in cat fur," she teased.

He looked up at her then. He noticed her nervous smile, the faint scar above her lip, her dark hair pulled back off her round face. He could see why other girls used to tease her. She seemed vulnerable somehow. He had known that the day he lied and took her money.

That's why I did it, he thought guiltily. *Jamee's right. Lark's too good for me.*

"Look, I gotta go." He stepped away from her. "Just keep it, all right?"

"I can't. But I got an idea," she said.

She reached into her book bag and pulled out a thick black marker. "You promise to pay me back, right?"

"Girl, I told you I would."

"Good," she said with a grin as she pulled off the marker cap and began drawing on his cast.

"What are you doin'?"

"You'll see. This is so you remember."

A few seconds later, she backed away. Fancy letters now covered a section of his cast.

"*T's Promise*," they read.

The letters were strong and angular, standing out bold and black against the cast like the murals painted on vacant buildings in the neighborhood.

"That looks good. Where'd you learn that?"

Her face lit up at his compliment. "Practice, I guess. I used to draw whenever I got mad at something. I guess I got mad a lot."

"Oh, so now you mad at me?"

"Not anymore," she admitted. "I know you're going to pay me back. I can tell," she replied, flashing him a smile that made his face warm.

"How come you so sure?"

"I don't know. I just am. Jamee

thinks you're just trying to play me again. But I told her she was wrong. You don't seem to be playin'. But if you are, I'll never forgive you. Not again," she said. "Here."

Lark handed Tyray the iPod. For a second, their hands brushed, and he could feel the warmth of her skin and the slight tremble in her fingers. He was surprised at how much her threat bothered him.

He slipped the iPod into his sweatshirt pocket and covered up his cast. The hallway was emptying. He remembered his father and how he had to go straight home after school. Already he was late.

"I really gotta go. My dad's gonna kill me," he said, turning away from her. "I'ma pay you back, though."

"You better. You promised," she said, gently tapping his cast and grinning back at him.

There was no way he would let her down, no matter what anyone said, not even Dad.

Tyray glanced twice at his cast as he followed his usual route home, rushing past Bluford's blacktop courts and cutting through the SuperFoods lot to Union Street. He knew if he kept the pace he would be home on time.

In the afternoon sun, with Lark's smile on his mind, Tyray thought the area seemed nothing like it had that ghostly morning with Dad. A young woman with a stroller crossed the street to Graham's. A few Bluford students walked nearby. The heavy scent of hamburgers from nearby Phat Burger filled the air. Tyray wanted to stop in, but he had no money and no time. That's when he noticed a "Help Wanted" sign posted on the door.

"Don't forget to get Bug's cheeseburger," someone called out.

Tyray turned to see a golden Nissan sedan. It was parked along the curb just a half a block ahead. Its chrome rims sparkled beneath dark tinted windows. Two kids stood next to it. One was a young boy he had never seen before, maybe a third or fourth grader. But the other was an older light-skinned boy with a wiry build. He had yelled out to someone who just slipped inside Phat Burger. Tyray knew his face.

They had met on 43rd Street. He was the guy who told Tyray to come to the lot in the middle of the night to pick up his gun. Tyray did what the boy said and got beaten up and robbed. The money stolen that night was Lark's.

Tyray froze in the middle of the side-walk. His heart started pounding. His hands tingled. He knew he had to get home, that he should just walk away. He could almost hear Mr. Mitchell urging him to do just that. But he couldn't stop himself.

"Yo, whatchu doin' here?" Tyray yelled.

The kid turned. Immediately his eyes narrowed. Tyray could see that he recognized him too.

"Man, you're the one that took my money!" Tyray growled. "Give it back."

"I didn't take no money from you. Whatchu talkin' 'bout?"

Tyray rushed to the car and moved right to the boy's face. The younger kid stepped back and ran off. Tyray ignored him.

"Don't lie to me! You told me to meet you, and I got jumped. Now give me my money back before I bust your face."

Tyray's pulse throbbed in his neck. He knew he had to go home, but he couldn't walk away from the kid who set

41

him up, especially not after seeing Lark.

"Look, *I* didn't take your money," the kid said, looking at Tyray's broken arm. "And if I was you, I'd get outta here 'cause you in over your head right now."

"Just give me my money!" Tyray shouted.

"I ain't givin' you nothin'. Now get outta my face!" the boy said, shoving Tyray back. He stumbled on the curb and his cast thudded against the Nissan. Tyray regained his footing and charged back just as a blur appeared at his side.

THUNK!

Pain exploded into Tyray's ribs, making him double over. He barely realized he had been hit before another blow hammered down on the back of his head. He slammed to the ground, scraping the side of his face on the curb. Warren's iPod flew from his pocket.

"See?" the boy said, standing over him with his hands balled up into fists, ready to strike. "Whatchu gonna do now, huh? You shoulda listened to me!"

Tyray looked up to see Jupiter James leaning over him. His saggy jeans were gathered over heavy boots that were just inches from Tyray's face.

"You again?" Jupiter mocked. "What's

42

wrong? You forgot what happened last time?"

"That's enough, Joop! C'mon. I already told you I don't want no trouble around here," said a different voice, older and deeper than the others.

"This ain't trouble," Jupiter replied. "*He* the one that started it, right Keenan?"

The light-skinned boy nodded and spit on the ground just inches from Tyray.

Tyray was stunned. Just like Dad said, the crew from 43rd Street was in his neighborhood. Even more surprising was the man standing behind Jupiter smoking a cigarette and wearing a black leather jacket. It was Londell, Jupiter's big brother. Tyray thought he was locked up at Cliffside Prison like Warren. Everyone knew he had been involved in a shooting last year where Roylin Bailey, Amberlynn's older brother, got grazed by a bullet. How could he be out so soon?

Tyray grabbed his ribs and sat up. He felt as if he was going to vomit.

"Next time this won't be the only thing you lose," Jupiter said, leaning over and picking up the iPod.

"No, you can't take that!" Tyray charged. "That's my brother's."

"I don't see his name on it," Joop mocked, slipping it into his pocket and moving toward the car. "You see a name on it, Kee?"

"Yeah, it says *Joop,*" Keenan replied, laughing.

"No! That's my brother's!" Tyray repeated. "He in Cliffside. C'mon, give it back!"

Jupiter stopped for a second. Londell turned at the mention of the prison.

"Who's your brother?" he asked.

"Warren Hobbs. You know him?"

"*Warren Hobbs?!*" A smug grin washed across Londell's face. "You mean *the Prof?* You're *his* little brother?" he said with a mean laugh.

"Who's *the Prof?*" Keenan asked.

"Just a fool who needs an education about how things really work out here," Londell said, starting the car. "Your brother can't protect you. He can't even protect himself."

"Whatchu mean?" Tyray asked, pulling himself up off the ground.

"C'mon," Londell urged. The crew crowded into the Nissan. Londell glanced at his cell phone and tossed his cigarette butt at Tyray's feet.

"Be careful who you're messin' with next time unless you want that other arm broke," he warned. He then gunned the accelerator and the Nissan roared off, leaving Tyray in a cloud of smoke.

"No!" Tyray groaned, rising to his feet as the car tore off.

People on the corner watched, but no one said a word. A man passed by in a gray sedan looking right at him but didn't stop. The young woman with the baby stroller rushed away as if she were scared of him.

Tyray rubbed his cheek and saw a smear of blood on his fingers from where he had hit the concrete. Outrage and disbelief warred inside him. He had been robbed again, twice by the same people. And they even knew his brother.

"He can't even protect himself."

What did that mean? What had happened to Warren? Tyray stomped the curb and cursed. He wished he still had the gun. He pictured himself aiming it at Jupiter, making him give back everything he stole. Then he would turn it on Londell and find out the truth about Warren.

But he knew it was all a stupid fantasy. The reality was that he was alone

45

on the sidewalk, bleeding.

And the guys who jumped him were free.

And Warren was locked up and in danger.

And his father hated him.

And no one seemed to care if he had his skull stomped right there on the street.

Tyray felt cursed as he stared back at the strangers who ignored him. It took all his strength not to scream.

Chapter 4

"You're late," Mom called as Tyray opened the front door.

He was relieved to hear the running faucet and the clatter of dishes in the sink. It meant his mother was in the kitchen and couldn't see his face. He darted straight to the bathroom.

"You shoulda' been here at 3:15. It's almost 4:00. Where you been?" she asked. It was one of the two days each week she got home early from Cottonwood Court Nursing Home, where she worked as a medical assistant. Dad wouldn't be home for another hour.

"I met with Mr. Mitchell. He wanted to talk about my English assignment," Tyray lied, locking the bathroom door and looking in the mirror. A thumb-sized scrape ran along his jaw. He knew

47

he couldn't hide it from her, but it almost didn't matter. His mind was spinning with what happened and what he had just learned.

Warren was in trouble.

Tyray left the bathroom and walked to the kitchen. Mom's back was to him, and she was mumbling, half to him and half to herself.

"So help me, Tyray. I hope you're not lying again. If we have to, we'll ground you until you're twenty-one—"

"Mom, how come you and Dad don't visit Warren no more?"

She turned. Her eyes fixed on his face, and her jaw dropped. A bowl slipped from her fingers and banged into the counter.

"What happened to your face? Who did this to you, baby?"

"It ain't no big thing. I was rushing to get home on time and slipped, that's all."

His mother examined him closely, touching the raw skin on his cheek. He winced and pulled away from her.

"You didn't answer me. How come you and Dad never go to Cliffside? You should see him," he said, the worry building in his chest. "Maybe I could come, too."

"Tyray, why are you bringing this up right now?"

"Because it's been over a year since they took him away. We ain't heard from him in months. What if something happened?"

"What are you talking about?" Mom asked, peering into his eyes. "Who have you been talking to?"

"No one," Tyray answered quickly, trying to stay calm. He couldn't tell her he had spoken to Londell James. That would only make things worse. "I'm just sayin', you know, it's been a long time. It ain't right that you cut him off."

"Cut him off? We never cut him off."

"Yes, you did. You act like he don't even exist. Dad gets mad whenever I say his name," Tyray said.

Mom took a deep breath and rubbed her temples.

"There's a lot you don't know, Tyray."

"What do you mean?"

"Look, I'm not going to go into it all now. Your father said—"

"I don't care what he said, Ma. He don't do nothin' but yell and complain all the time. He don't even care what happens," Tyray huffed, feeling a wave of bitterness as he spoke.

"No, Tyray. You got him all wrong. He cares. It's just he's . . ." Mom paused as if she was about to say something but then changed her mind. "He doesn't always know how to show it."

"Yeah, right."

"*Excuse me?*" Mom's eyes flashed with anger. "I know you *think* you know everything right now, but you don't, okay? Your father and I fought hard for Warren. But he didn't want to listen. All he wanted to do was hang out with his boys or that girlfriend, Chantel. Then one night he holds up a store!" she exclaimed, shaking her head as she spoke. "I still can't believe it."

Tyray couldn't either. He remembered how Warren changed during his junior year of high school, becoming secretive and irritable. Sometimes he stayed out all night, despite Dad's yelling. Once Dad threatened to kick him out if he didn't start listening. Warren promised he would, but a few days later the police came.

Tyray had been in a deep sleep when the pounding started.

BANG! BANG! BANG!

The blows were so strong, they knocked the pictures off the wall. Tyray heard them smash to the ground just outside his bedroom.

Dad had rushed down the hall, but he was powerless to stop the officers from shouldering him aside. Tyray covered his eyes as piercing white lights flooded his room and then beamed down the hallway.

Mom shrieked, and Dad yelled.

"Not my son. He didn't do nothin'! You're makin' a mistake," he had said over and over again.

Tyray still remembered the muffled sounds of men's voices coming from his brother's room. Then a sickening thud shook the floor. He had rushed to the edge of the hallway to see the policemen yank Warren out in handcuffs.

"Tell them you didn't do it, Warren," Dad pleaded. *"Tell them the truth, boy!"*

Warren had stumbled forward, his eyes wide with fear. He glanced back at them for an instant.

"I'm sorry," was all he said before they forced him outside.

Tyray felt a raw gush of anger whenever he remembered that night. It had never really gone away, a scar that wouldn't heal. He would feel it when he looked in Warren's empty room or noticed

51

the scuff marks where the officers' shoes scraped the floor. He even felt it at Bluford sometimes, a rage that had fueled his attacks on others, including Darrell.

"I know it hurts to hear this," Mom said, snapping him out of his thoughts, "but Warren brought this problem on himself."

Tyray scratched at his broken wrist, feeling the anger swirl in him again.

"But that don't mean you should just forget him," he blurted. No matter what Mom said, he still couldn't understand why they had given up on Warren.

"No one *forgot* him!" Mom yelled. "I think about him every day. I brought that boy into this world and raised him right so he could make a good life for himself. There's no way I could forget him."

"Then visit him, Mom," Tyray said, feeling his voice shake. "And take me with you."

Mom looked at Tyray for a minute, as if she were debating what to say. "Listen, Tyray. We never told you, but the last time we went to Cliffside, Warren got into an argument with your father. We started talking about responsibility, and he got upset and started cursin', tellin' us we don't understand nothin'. He went back to his cell and told the guard he didn't want to see us again. Since then he hasn't answered my letters. What are we supposed to do?" she asked, her voice quivering. "Go on, tell me, since you got all the answers."

Tyray sucked his teeth as Mom's words slowly sank in. He hadn't gotten a letter from Warren in over six months. Maybe his brother was angry at them, but what did that have to do with him? And no matter what, it didn't change what Londell said. Warren could be in trouble and no one would know it.

"Maybe I can go see him myself," he suggested.

He noticed his mother's face change for an instant, as if he had said something that made sense. But just as quickly it changed back.

"No, Tyray. This is a prison, not a park. They don't just let kids go walking around. You gotta be on their list and have proper ID. You're supposed to have an adult with you, too. Besides, I don't want you to go there. It's not a place I want you to see."

"C'mon, Ma. If he don't want to see you, maybe he'll see me. At least then we'll know he's okay," he said, struggling to hide his worries.

"Boy, I don't know what's gotten into you. Warren's been gone over a year, and you've never acted like this." Mom inspected his face again, as if she thought he had a fever.

Tyray glanced at the family pictures hanging on the wall: one from Christmas when Tyray was ten, the other from a barbecue they had on Warren's fifteenth birthday. Warren had a corny smile because Tyray had teased him about his new girlfriend, Chantel, seconds before the photo was taken. Warren hated the picture, but Mom had insisted on hanging it.

Looking at his brother, Tyray felt the sadness tugging at him again. He couldn't tell Mom everything that was on his mind, but he couldn't keep quiet, either.

"I miss him, Ma." The words almost caught in his throat. He could feel them in his bones.

Mom sighed. Tyray knew she was watching him. He wished he could stop the thoughts racing in his head and tell her what really haunted him.

I'm scared.

I think something bad happened to Warren.

You shoulda seen the look on Londell's face.

Instead, he scuffed his shoe against the cracked linoleum on the kitchen floor.

"Tyray, I know you're upset. But it's gonna be okay. You hear me?" she said. "What you need to do is worry about the things *you* can control, so you don't end up in the same place."

You don't even understand, Tyray wanted to say. Instead he nodded, and his mother kept on talking, listing things he should be doing. Homework. Getting involved in school activities. Going to church. Her voice droned on, and he stopped listening. Finally, she hugged him. Her touch made him sadder, even more alone. But he didn't fight it.

"What's this?" she asked when she released him a few seconds later. She was pointing to the words on his cast.

T's promise.

"Nothin'. Just something some girl wrote on there." He remembered Lark and the debt he still owed her.

"Some girl?"

"It's nothin', Ma," he replied, covering the cast. Outside, he heard an engine rumble and knew Dad was home from work. There was no way he wanted to talk with him around. They would end up arguing like always.

"What's your promise?"

"Nothin', Ma. Don't worry about it."

Tyray turned and went down the hall to his bedroom and closed the door.

In his mind, Londell's voice kept echoing.

"Warren can't even protect himself."

Chapter 5

Tyray arrived at Bluford Monday morning to find Jamee and Amberlynn waiting for him at his locker. The scowl on Jamee's face cut through the crowded hallway like a spotlight.

Girl, that better not be for me, he thought as he approached them. *Your mug is the last one I want to see right now.*

"Why you lyin' to her?" Jamee asked, her eyes darting to the scab on his jaw and then to the writing on his cast.

"Huh?"

"You know you're just using her," Jamee grumbled. "I told you she's my friend, and I don't want to see you hurt her again."

"Seriously, Jamee. You need to step back, 'cause I can't take this—"

"Listen to me," Amberlynn cut in.

"Lark is fragile, okay. There's a lot that's goin' on in her family, and we don't wanna see you makin' it worse."

Tyray's head was spinning. The news of his brother had haunted him all weekend. He wasn't ready for something to threaten Lark.

"Whatchu mean? Is she okay?"

"What we mean is you shouldn't be makin' *promises* you can't keep," Jamee snapped, glaring at his cast.

Amberlynn stepped in before Tyray could respond. "What Jamee means is Lark likes you, Tyray. She really does."

"Yeah, which is why you should just walk away now, because we know you don't care nothin' about her," Jamee hissed.

Tyray felt an urge to shove a book in Jamee's mouth so she couldn't talk. He was about to curse her out when another voice cut him off.

"What's everybody doing here?"

Tyray turned to see Lark. He took a deep breath and swallowed his words.

"We were just talking, that's all," Jamee said, her voice a bit high and unnatural.

"Yeah, we got a quiz in Mr. Mitchell's class, and Jamee thinks I'ma fail it, but

I'ma prove her wrong," Tyray said, trying his best to sound serious. Lark flashed him a smile. He saw the tiny scar over her lip. He felt bad lying to her again.

Overhead, the bell rang and the girls moved down the hallway together. "See you at lunch," Lark said with a weak smile.

The day had barely started, and already Tyray had a headache. But as he rubbed his forehead, Lark's words blazed on his forearm.

At lunchtime, Tyray noticed Lark's friends watching him as he grabbed a seat at an empty table in the far corner of the cafeteria. He was still angry at Jamee for what she had said to him, and yet he almost respected her, too. She was just looking out for Lark. He wished he had friends ready to fight for him. But he was alone, even in his own family.

So was Warren, he figured. Londell's words had gnawed at him all weekend.

He forced down a few bites of the cafeteria's leathery cheeseburger when Lark arrived at his table. There was that smile again. The tiny scar. The enormous book bag sprinkled with cat fur.

"Can I sit with you?" she asked. He

could see her looking at his cheek, but she didn't mention it.

"Nah," he said bitterly, pointing to the empty table. "All my friends'll get jealous if you do that."

"Yeah, well they're just gonna have to deal with it," she said with a grin as she dropped her book bag. It hit the ground with a heavy thud.

"Whatchu carrying in there? Bricks?" Tyray asked.

"Books," she said, looking a bit embarrassed. "I just got a new one from the library."

Tyray rolled his eyes as she fished out a thick hardbound book with a black and red cover. He read the title. *Moonlight.*

"What's it about?"

"Vampires," she admitted sheepishly.

"Vampires?"

"Yeah, I just love these books. There are, like, eight of them. I can't put them down. They even have a movie coming out next month."

"For real?" He flipped through the pages. "Why you like 'em so much?" He had never felt that way about any book.

"You sound just like my little brother, Kyle," she said with an odd look on her face. "Well, for one, when I'm reading I get away. You ever wanna just get away?"

"Every day," Tyray muttered, remembering what Amberlynn said about Lark's home.

"Plus they're fun. You remind me of someone in here," she said, putting the book back in the bag.

"Oh man, I'm not even gonna try to guess what that means."

"I'm not tellin'," she said, almost blushing. "You're just gonna have to read it if you wanna find out."

"I don't know 'bout that," Tyray admitted. "That's, like, five hundred pages."

"That's fine. It's my secret, then," she said, flashing that smile again.

Tyray studied her face. Now that he knew her, she seemed so different than the shy girl others talked about and laughed at. Yes, she was quiet at first, but once he got to know her, she was also funny and smart. And yet she seemed to be hiding something, too.

"So what do you need to get away from?" Tyray asked.

In an instant, her face clouded over. "You don't want to go there," she said, gently touching the scar on her lip. "Anyway, you should read the book. I'm serious. You might like it."

Lark was silent for a few seconds. Tyray noticed that she avoided looking at him. In the distance, over her shoulder, he could see Jamee and Amberlynn watching them.

"What about you?" she asked finally, breaking the silence. "What are you trying to escape?"

"Please," he said. "You ain't even tryin' to hear that story. If it was a book, it'd be, like, two thousand pages."

"I'm listening."

"Well, maybe start with a vacation from those two," he joked, pointing to Jamee and Amberlynn.

"They're just looking out for me. I know that's why they were at your locker this morning. By the way, your lie wasn't any good. You'd never talk to Jamee. Especially not about schoolwork."

For the first time in weeks, Tyray almost smiled. "I thought I had you fooled," he said.

"Nah, you're gonna have to try a little harder next time," Lark replied with a weak smile.

Tyray glanced at her and the loyal friends she had just a few feet away. He knew they didn't like him sitting with her, that they wanted to keep her safe.

And maybe they were right. Maybe he was dangerous to people like them.

But not to Lark.

Looking at her scar and the sadness hiding behind her eyes, he knew he wouldn't hurt her again. Instead, he wanted to honor his promise and stop what haunted her. But how? He forced down another leathery bite of his cheeseburger when an idea hit him.

A way to pay her back.

Tyray headed straight to Phat Burger after school. The black and orange sign from the other day still hung in the window. *Help Wanted.*

He knew he had to be quick. He opened the familiar glass door and stepped inside. The air was a soupy mix of grease and fried onions. Tyray loved the smell. He headed straight to the line and waited. Up until recently, he would look down at the people behind the counter flipping burgers in their corny uniforms and visors. But that was before he was desperate for money.

"Can I help you?" grumbled a large dark-skinned woman behind the counter. Tyray recognized her from when he and Rodney used to go there after school.

They would joke about the way she sweated whenever it was busy.

"Yo, she gonna drip in your fries," Rodney used to say.

"Yeah, girl, hold that secret sauce," Tyray would say, cracking up in the line as he spent Darrell's money.

Now he hoped she didn't remember him.

"Uh, I saw your sign outside. I am lookin' for a job," he said. He saw a nametag on her chest that read *Selma.* It was the first time he had ever noticed her name.

Selma sucked her teeth and looked down at his cast. She scowled slightly before reaching under the counter and sliding a rumpled application toward him.

"Next," she huffed.

"Wait," Tyray said. "What do I do?"

"Fill it out." There was an edge to her voice. He knew she remembered him.

"And then give it to you?"

"Mmm hmm. But you ain't gonna get hired, not with that cast on your arm. You can't cook with *that,*" she said, straightening her visor. *"Next!"*

Tyray took the application and sat down in a nearby booth. *What was the point,* he figured. He knew Selma was going to throw his application away as soon as he finished it. He was about to crumple the paper himself when he heard a deep rattling cough. The sound made him freeze. He knew exactly who it was.

Bones.

The wiry man crept to the front of the line and ordered. Tyray hadn't seen him since he had sold him the gun. He folded the application and shoved it in his back pocket. He wanted to run out.

"Yo, little man," said the voice as rough as crushed concrete.

Tyray shuddered. Bones grabbed a greasy bag from Selma and came toward him. His skin stretched like worn paper over his skull.

"Whatchu doin' here, little brother? What happened to your face?"

"Nothin'," Tyray answered. Just seeing Bones made his insides tremble. "I gotta go. I'm late already."

"Late for what?" Bones asked. He reached a long finger in the bag and pulled out some French fries. "C'mon. Let's go outside."

Tyray got up and headed out with Bones following him. "I really gotta go. I'm grounded. My pops wants me home right away."

Bones swallowed heavily and dug out more French fries. "You didn't do it, did you?" he asked, examining Tyray with cold unblinking eyes as they slowly walked up the block.

Tyray knew exactly what he was talking about: whether he had used the gun. Bones had warned him about the gun the day he had sold it to him.

"Boy, you got a choice to make. This ain't on my hands," he had said. *"If you take that dude out, his face is gonna be with you until the day you die . . . be the last face you see at night before you go to sleep. Be the last face you see before you die."* Tyray had ignored him at first, but later, when he stared at Darrell in the alley, he started to understand.

"No," Tyray admitted, suddenly feeling embarrassed.

"You get scared?" Bones asked with a cold smile, ketchup dripping from his fingers.

"Nah! I wasn't scared. It ain't like that," Tyray blurted, his voice louder than he had meant it to be. "I just . . . couldn't do it," he admitted.

"'Cause you was scared," Bones repeated with a raspy chuckle.

"No, I wasn't!"

"So what was it then?"

"Man, what's your problem?" Tyray yelled. "When I saw him lying there cryin', I couldn't, okay? And then I . . ." He paused and remembered the final instant he had turned the gun on himself instead. "Look, I don't wanna talk about it. I'm late. I ain't got time for this—"

"Boy, look at my face! I'm dyin'. Don't talk to me about *time*!" he barked, and he began coughing, a fit that ended with him spitting something rust colored onto the curb.

Tyray cringed. He didn't want to be near the sickly man with his wheeze and piercing eyes. And yet he couldn't just walk away.

"Years ago, I'da busted on you for bein' a coward. Today I'd say you was just bein' smart," Bones said, squinting at Tyray as if he were trying to read something he couldn't quite see. "I'm kinda surprised, though. You had that look in your eye. I thought you was gonna go through with it." He paused, taking a heavy breath. "That's all right. I don't need no more blood on my hands." He tossed a fry aside as if it disgusted him. "Not with where I'm goin'."

Tyray squirmed. "Man, I'm sorry,"

he said. "But I really need to go. My dad already grounded me, and I was supposed to be home twenty minutes ago."

A car passed by, and Bones crumpled up the bag of French fries.

"That's right. Old Gil Hobbs will get mad if you're late, right? That man's got issues, but I can't blame him after what he's been through," he said knowingly.

Tyray wasn't sure what he meant. Then Bones's face suddenly grew serious.

"You seen your brother since he got locked up?" he asked.

Tyray froze. Bones's cheeks were slightly sunken, and his hands were gnarled with veins, but his eyes smoldered with invisible fire. Warren had mentioned him a few times long ago, but Tyray hadn't expected the skinny man to bring up Warren. Did he know something about what Londell said?

"Nah. Why?"

Bones stared at him for a few seconds. "You see him, let him know I was askin' 'bout him, y'hear me? Tell him I'm sorry."

Something about Bones's voice was strange, the way his last words hung in the air.

"He ain't in trouble, is he?" Tyray

asked, unable to hide his thoughts. "Londell James said—"

"Londell James? Whatchu talkin' to him for?" Bones's face tightened into a sneer. For an instant, Tyray saw his teeth, yellowed and crooked. They almost looked like fangs.

Tyray explained how he had been jumped and how Jupiter stole Warren's iPod. He also mentioned how Londell threatened him.

"I don't know how he got out of jail so quick," Tyray grumbled. "Everyone knows what he did."

Bones scowled and shook his head as if Tyray had said something silly. "'Cause ain't nobody wanna snitch on him. Everybody's too scared, so the police can't do nothin'. You got any sense in your head, you'll stay away from him, too," Bones said.

"Dude robbed me twice," Tyray grumbled. "And he knows somethin' about Warren."

"So whatchu gonna do about it?"

Tyray hated that he had no good answer. He shrugged in frustration. "Nothin', I guess."

"That's right. You stay away from the James brothers, y'hear me? You got somethin' none of us got. You better keep it," Bones said.

"Man, what are you sayin'?"

Bones shook his head. "Visit your brother, and ask him. He'll tell you. Don't forget to tell him what I said," he huffed, walking down the street toward the corner.

"Man, I can't just go see him. My dad won't let me. Besides, I hear you gotta have an adult with you and some paper-work or somethin' like that."

Bones stopped and turned back to him. Tyray thought he heard him curs-ing under his breath. From a distance, his face looked almost like a skull. And yet the skinny man was scratching his chin thoughtfully, as if he was planning something.

"You wanna go, you meet me next Sunday morning. 10:00. Right out here at the bus station. I'll get you there."

"For real?" Tyray asked.

Bones slipped around the corner without a word, disappearing like a shadow.

Chapter 6

"Where is he?!" Dad barked.

Tyray braced himself as he stood outside the front door. He could hear his father yelling as he reached the cement slab driveway alongside their house. Tyray wished he could just keep walking. Instead, he forced himself to open the door. He grabbed the half-completed application from his pocket just to prove to his father where he was.

"Boy, you better have a good excuse," Dad hollered. "You think we were kidding when we told you what time to be home?"

"No," Tyray said. His head felt ready to burst with thoughts of Warren, Lark, and Londell. Now Dad was just adding to the pressure. He rose from the couch and approached Tyray.

"Give him a chance to explain, Gil,"

said Mom, looking worried.

"I'm tired of giving him chances. Seems the only time he ever listens is when I knock some sense into him. I'm beginnin' to think that's what he needs right now."

Tyray shook his head in frustration. He couldn't stand the sound of Dad's yelling. Before he could explain where he had been, he heard the angry reply escape his lips.

"Man, that's all you ever wanna do anyway," Tyray mumbled.

"What's that?" Dad asked, stepping closer, fire in his eyes. "You got somethin' to say to me, boy? Go on. Let's hear it!"

Tyray knew if he said anything, Dad would slap him. He had done it before. But with everything on his mind, he almost didn't care. Besides, he knew what Dad thought. For days, Dad's words had ricocheted through Tyray's mind like bullets.

"He ain't no good . . . He ain't nothing but trouble . . ."

"Why don't you both just sit down?" Mom suggested.

Tyray knew he should listen, but he couldn't. He had tried to do the right thing. Find a way to pay back Lark. Get

72

a job. Visit his brother. But Dad didn't care. He just kept coming.

"No, I don't wanna sit down!" Tyray said, his heart pounding.

"Excuse me?"

Part of Tyray was scared, but another part couldn't hold back his frustration. "All you ever do is yell, Dad. No matter what I do, it ain't good enough. You wanna hit me? Go ahead. There ain't no use talking to you anyway."

"Gil," Mom protested. "Don't do this—"

SMACK!

The back of Dad's hand swung round and caught Tyray in the mouth, snapping his head to the side and splitting his lip.

"What else you gotta say?" Dad barked.

"You see!" Tyray cried out in outrage, trying to raise his arms to block him. "You don't even wanna listen—"

CRACK!

Gil Hobbs struck again, a bit harder this time. Tyray hit the wall and fell to the ground, dropping the paper. He wanted to raise his fists at his father, but it was as if invisible chains held his arms down. It was a line he couldn't cross.

"I hate you, Dad!" Tyray cried, tears of rage and hurt in his eyes. "I hate you!"

"That's enough, Gil!" Mom screamed, darting between them.

"How do you know it's enough? Huh?! Maybe if I'da been tougher on Warren, he wouldn't be where he is now," Dad huffed. He tried to step around her, but she held him, locking her arms around his.

"He's had enough," Mom repeated, looking Dad in the eye. "It wasn't right when your daddy did it to you, so why are you doing it to him?"

Dad ignored her comment and glared at Tyray. "You don't have to like me, but you *will* respect me!" he hollered over Mom's shoulder. "And you will follow the rules of this house. You understand?"

For a second no one moved. The dining room was silent except for the sound of Dad's breathing. It was like the alley after the gun blast.

Tyray tasted blood in his mouth and saw tiny red droplets on his cast. He nodded.

Dad took a deep breath and stepped outside. Mom rushed to the kitchen and put some ice cubes in a towel. She handed it to Tyray and tried to help him up, but he shrugged away from her.

"Don't touch me!" he fumed, angry at

74

the tears in his eyes. Tears for all that was wrong between them, for all that was wrong with his life. He escaped to his bedroom, slamming the door behind him.

Hours later, as the darkness gradually swallowed his room, Tyray's mind filled with one thought.

He wished Darrell had been a little slower, that the bullet had not missed.

Tyray crept through the dark alley once again. The rain was falling, coating everything in a silvery sheen. The gun was back in his hand, heavy and warm.

And then he heard it. The thud of a car door closing. The low cough of an engine starting not far away.

He jogged toward the sound. It had to be close. Just up ahead.

The sound of the engine grew louder. He could smell the exhaust in the air. He turned the corner and was blinded by headlights. But he knew what it was.

The golden Nissan.

Its lights cut the darkness like the flashlights in his room a year ago. As his eyes adjusted, he could just make out the silhouette of the driver, and he noticed the dim orange glow of a cigarette. He was sure it was Londell behind the wheel.

Somewhere far off he heard a woman cry, but he didn't care.

He glanced to his left and realized he was on the blacktop lot near Bluford High School. Lark and Jamee were sitting on the front steps of the school watching him. Darrell was there, too. Mr. Mitchell shook his head as if he was disappointed.

To his right, the lot stretched out before him, pocked with shallow holes just like the ones he and Dad had searched to find the gun.

Suddenly, the car's wheels chirped on the asphalt. The Nissan lurched toward him.

He tried to raise the gun, but his movement was slowed somehow. It was like the night in the alley. He just wasn't fast enough. Already the car bore down on him. He glanced on either side, but there was nowhere to run.

"No!" he screamed. But the car did not stop.

In horror, he felt the impact of the sedan striking his legs. His torso came crashing down on the hood. His cast shattered. Lark's writing broke apart, and for an instant, Tyray saw the driver, his lips pressed tight together, his eyes glaring with anger.

It wasn't Londell. It was Dad.

Tyray screamed. He sat upright in his bed, covered in sweat. He turned to his clock and saw the red numbers. It was 3:17 in the morning, and his window was dark except for the glow of a streetlight filtering through the corners of his shade. The house was silent for a moment, but then Tyray heard the shuffle of footsteps. A second later, there was a click, and his room was flooded with harsh electric light.

Tyray squinted.

"What's wrong?" Dad asked. "I heard you hollering."

"Nothin'. I just had a bad dream, that's all," he said with a shiver. The memories of their argument flooded back into his mind.

"You sure you all right? What'd you dream about?"

Tyray didn't know what to say. Not after the fight they'd had or what he had seen moments earlier. He kept picturing his father's steely expression as he drove the car right through him.

"Nothin'," Tyray said. "Just something dumb about school."

His father took a deep breath and shook his head. In the harsh light, his face seemed gray and older. Bags hung from beneath his eyes, and there were creases in his forehead. He looked as if he hadn't slept at all. Had he even gone to bed?

"It's late. Go on back to sleep," he said, clicking off the light.

The floor creaked as his father stepped back into the hallway. Tyray heard him pause for a moment and sigh quietly before going back to his room and closing the door.

Tyray stretched back into his bed and tried to erase the nightmare from his mind. In the darkness, he could still see Dad's glare as he made the car destroy him.

The next morning, Tyray waited in his room until Dad left for work.

At breakfast, he sat motionless and dazed, barely touching his cereal. He could feel Mom staring at him, but his thoughts kept racing.

"Your father didn't mean what he said last night," Mom said finally as Tyray stared into his bowl.

"I don't care," he replied, stirring

78

the milk and then pushing the whole bowl away.

Londell, Lark, Warren, Bones. Their faces flashed through his mind like lightning from an approaching storm.

"Tyray, you have to eat, baby," she said nudging it back in front of him.

"Don't call me *baby!*" Tyray snapped and shoved the bowl with his cast, sending it to the floor. Mom's eyes grew wide in surprise.

"Tyray!"

"I don't want it, okay?" Tyray hissed. "I don't want nothin' from any of you!"

"Now you pick that up, y'hear me?" Mom yelled.

Tyray's head was throbbing. He felt an urge to hit her, to strike back at everything that was wrong in his life, though it wasn't her fault. Instead, he turned away and put his face in his hands, so he wouldn't have to see her. His pulse pounded like a hammer in his head.

"I'm goin', Ma. None of y'all are gonna stop me."

"Goin' where?"

"To see Warren," he replied, throwing his hands down and staring her in the eye. "I need to see him."

His mother shook her head as if she didn't know what to do with him. "Is that what this is all about? Warren?"

Tyray clenched his jaw and fought back the urge to scream. There was too much happening. He was being pulled in too many directions, and there was no way he could explain it all to her. He was sure she was going to lecture him. If she did, he would lose it. Rage boiled in his chest, ready to explode.

Mom didn't say a word. Instead, she stared at him for several long seconds.

"How you gonna get in there? Huh?" she asked finally. "You need papers, Tyray, and an adult and—"

"I don't know!" he boomed, cutting her off and banging his cast on the table. "But I'll figure it out, okay. I got no choice, Ma. Y'hear me? I gotta do this," he insisted, turning away from the pained look on her face. He knew he could never mention Bones.

Tyray felt his mother staring at him. He heard her pick up the spilled bowl and place it in the sink. Then she sighed wearily as if something inside had just given up.

"C'mon," she said, her voice different from before. "You'll need this if you go."

Mom led him down the hall. He stood at the edge of his parents' bedroom, while she grabbed a small silver key from her dresser. Then she opened her closet. Inside was a gray metal file cabinet he had never noticed. She opened it with the key and pulled out something bundled in a plastic bag and placed it next to her while she rifled through some papers.

Tyray almost fell over. He was almost certain what was in the bag. It was the gun. *His* gun. It had to be. Dad hadn't turned it in.

He didn't say a word as Mom dug through a thick stack of papers and official-looking envelopes. A second later she pulled out two sheets and handed them to him. He glanced at the first one.

> *This note is to certify that Tyray Hobbs is an approved visitor for Warren Hobbs, inmate #321629 at Cliffside Correctional Facility.*

The second was a stamped sheet with the words "Visitation Form." It was dated from last year. At the bottom were a number of names, printed in Warren's handwriting.

Gilbert Hobbs
Elaine M. Hobbs
Tyray Hobbs
Chantel Williams

Tyray was surprised to see Chantel's name on the sheet. Tyray hadn't heard anyone mention her name since Warren was arrested.

"Take these, your school ID, and this," Mom said firmly, handing him a copy of his own birth certificate. "Visiting hours are weekends only. They won't let you in any other time. When you see him, tell him we love him. You hear me?" she added, wiping her eyes.

Tyray nodded. He was speechless.

"Now go," she said, turning away from him. "Don't be late for school."

Chapter 7

"Everyone, please clear your desks," announced Mr. Mitchell. "It's time for a quiz."

The class groaned. Tyray slouched back into his chair and stared at his worn copy of *Lord of the Flies*. He hadn't read past the second page. The last thing he wanted to do was read about a bunch of rich white kids in some jungle. What did that have to do with anything?

Tyray's face still ached from his fight with Dad. His mind kept racing over his talk with Mom, the prison forms hidden in his room, and Warren sitting alone in a cell a few hours away.

The quiz landed on his desk. Tyray wrote his name and glanced at the questions he knew he couldn't answer. Next to him, Tasha silently signaled to Janelle for an answer to item two. Janelle mimed answer choice *C*, careful to keep an eye on Mr. Mitchell. They were cheating.

Tyray had seen it countless times and never cared. But now, after everything, it suddenly annoyed him. Tasha and her friends would get another good grade while he would get an F. Then they'd act as if they were perfect and he was a loser. But it was all fake.

"You ain't no better than me," he mumbled to himself. At the bottom of the sheet were three essay questions. He had to answer one.

1. *Why do you think everyone picked on Piggy? Explain.*
2. *Even though they know it's wrong, many join in the violence. Why?*
3. *Would today's students behave the same as those in* Lord of the Flies? *Explain your answer.*

Tyray's head throbbed. He was weary from not sleeping. He knew there was no point trying to write about a book he didn't read, but the words "join in the violence" caught his eyes. Many sitting around him had been there in the cafeteria the day he and Darrell fought. He remembered the looks in their eyes as they cheered *"Fight! Fight! Fight!"* After Tyray's wrist cracked and started swelling, some snickered as if it was all a joke. They were quick to laugh again when he tried to give Lark the iPod. Some might even have seen his fight with Jupiter and Keenan, though no one bothered to help.

I don't need no book to tell me about violence. I been there, he thought to himself. Tyray grabbed his pen and jotted some words on his quiz sheet.

> People in this school are either cowards or animals. The animals travel in packs ready to gang up on you if they think it'll get them something. Popularity. Reputation. Whatever. It don't matter that it's not right cause it gets them what they want. The cowards are people that join the animals cause they are scared. They are afraid to stand up to them cause they know if they do, they'll be called a snitch or get jumped next time. I don't want to be neither. Any book that says this is realistic.

Tyray turned in his paper and slumped in his seat as Mr. Mitchell waited for everyone to finish. The teacher glanced at Tyray's sheet as he collected the rest of the quizzes. He then circled to the side of the room. Tyray knew by the look on his face that he was about to start another one of his discussions. Tyray rolled his eyes.

"Okay, so imagine you're on the island with the boys in this book. They begin to pick on the younger kids and then turn on Piggy. What do you think you would do? Be honest."

The class was silent. Tyray noticed Tasha and Janelle whisper something about Piggy being overweight. Then they both looked at Harold. The heavy boy was motionless in his seat, as if he was trying to hide.

"Well, for one, I wouldn't be goin' around cuttin' pigs heads off and smearin' blood everywhere. That's just nasty," said Jamee. A few students mumbled in agreement.

Tyray was surprised. The description didn't sound like any book Mr. Mitchell would assign. He glanced at the cover. An odd white face peered back at him. Leaves and branches were in his hair. Something next to the face was stained red. It looked like a body.

"For real, I think these kids are

messed up, Mr. Mitchell," said Rodney from the other side of the room. "Ain't none of us psycho like that." He snuck a quick glance at Tyray.

"Well maybe one of us is," whispered Janelle under her breath to Tasha.

Tyray knew it was an insult aimed at him, though he wasn't sure Janelle meant for him to hear it. He wanted to say something back to her, but he knew it would turn ugly if he did. Instead, he scratched at his cast and noticed Lark's writing. It had already faded slightly.

T's promise.

He imagined himself paying her back, looking at Lark's face as he handed her the money he had stolen. Maybe her smile would light up like it sometimes did when they talked, or maybe whatever haunted her would stop for a while. Either way, he would finally do something good, no matter what Dad said or his classmates thought. He held on to the image like a lifeline.

"Tyray?"

It was Mr. Mitchell's voice. He looked up to see the teacher staring at him.

"Huh?"

Some people snickered. Tasha smirked.

"You're on the island. You see kids

87

roughing up Piggy," he explained. "You think it's realistic that young people would behave this way?"

Tyray gazed at the teacher. He was certain Mr. Mitchell knew he hadn't read the book. Was he trying to embarrass him?

The entire class seemed to stop breathing as they waited for his answer. It was almost as if they wanted him to mess up, as if they were eager for another chance to kick him while he was down.

"Man, I don't know about no island," he huffed, feeling their stares crawl over him. "But I know people in school who do that. Some are here right now. Happens every day. Everybody knows it, but they just keepin' quiet 'cause they don't wanna snitch," he said, thinking of Tasha's quiz and then of Londell James. People everywhere were doing something wrong, and other people knew it but said nothing.

"I hope you ain't acting like you're any better?" Jamee said, looking over at Darrell. "Not after what you've done—"

"Easy, Jamee," Mr. Mitchell said, cautioning her.

Tyray sat up in his seat, ignoring the teacher.

"*I* ain't never said I didn't do nothin' wrong. But some of you are actin' like you're saints or somethin'," he snapped. "Who's gangin' up now? Huh? But it's all good. I don't need no little gang to hide behind," he said, unable to hide the bitterness in his voice. "I don't need none of y'all."

The class hushed as if Tyray's words sucked the air out of the room. Jamee's jaw dropped as if she couldn't believe what she had just heard. Tyray didn't care. He leaned back in his chair and stared down at his cast.

Mr. Mitchell nodded thoughtfully. "I never said talking about this would be easy. But it's important. It's how we learn from each other, so I ask that you show each other some respect. Now, according to Tyray, what we're reading isn't that different from our own school," he said holding his copy of *Lord of the Flies*. "What do the rest of you think? Is Bluford that rough?"

The room was quiet for several moments. Tyray squirmed, waiting for the class to end. Finally Darrell Mercer spoke up.

"It can be," he said, eyeing Tyray. "But not usually in class. It's what happens after class or in, like, the bathroom or the gym."

"Nah, it's rough everywhere," added Harold, without turning his head. Tyray had hardly ever heard him speak in class, even when other kids teased him.

Mr. Mitchell asked for more people to comment, but Tyray stopped listening. He'd had enough. All the talk didn't fix his problems at home. It didn't free Warren or stop Tyray from getting robbed. It didn't keep guys like Jupiter and Londell from messing up his neighborhood. It was all just a waste of time.

RING!

The bell blasted overhead. Tyray bolted from his desk, eager to leave.

"Tyray, can I speak with you a minute?" Mr. Mitchell asked, stopping him before he could reach the door.

Not again, Tyray thought.

"I don't wanna be late, Mr. Mitchell," he said, pretending to care about algebra.

The teacher stared at him. Tyray was sure he saw the marks on his cheek, his swollen lip. There was no way he could hide them.

"You okay?" he asked finally.

"Yeah, why you askin'?" Tyray grumbled, throwing the question back at him. "Look, I need to get to my next class. I got a quiz today."

"Tyray . . . is there something else going on at home or—"

"Like what? Whatchu think is goin' on, Mr. Mitchell?" Tyray snapped, looking at the teacher in his blue button-down shirt, khaki pants, and jungle-print tie. Tyray took a step toward the door.

"You're not alone, Tyray. There are people to talk to, like I mentioned before."

Just shut up, Mr. Mitchell, he wanted to say. *What do you know about anything?* His eyes locked on the stack of papers on the teacher's desk. Tasha's paper was on top. Mr. Mitchell had written the words "*See me*" in the corner in red ink.

"I don't need to talk to anyone, okay? I just need to get outta here," Tyray blurted.

"And go where?"

Tyray shrugged. Why wouldn't the teacher just leave him alone?

"I hate to break it to you, Tyray, but there are a lot of places in the world worse than school. I hope you never have to see them. Ask Warren. I know he'd agree with me."

Tyray looked up at the mention of his brother. "Whatchu know about him?"

"I remember him well, Tyray. He was a smart young man with a promising future. The last thing he'd want is for his little brother to end up where he is now. School isn't perfect, but it's the best way to avoid that path. But you gotta do your part, Tyray. I can't do it for you."

"Man, whatever," Tyray replied, gently kicking the edge of the desk.

"Look, Tyray. We don't get to pick the hand we're dealt. But we still have to play our cards. You hear me? You got choices. Everyday you're making them, whether you know it or not. Right now you're choosing to fail my class, and you're pushing everyone away. I suggest a different choice. Do your work in here. Talk to someone. Your description of this school isn't right. Not everyone here is mean. Some of them would be friends with you in a second if you let them." The teacher looked at Tyray's cast as he spoke. "Find good people and open up to them."

For an instant, Tyray imagined school without everyone hating or looking down at him. He couldn't believe that path was open to him. It was for Darrell with his wrestler friends or maybe even Harold with his grandmother who watched him like a hawk.

But not for me, Tyray thought, remembering what Dad had said.

"Man, you don't get it," Tyray answered, trying to clear the image from his mind. "I don't need them. I don't care what they think."

"I hear you, Tyray. I get it. You don't need anyone, right?" he asked, crossing his arms and nodding for a second. "But let's be real. How's that workin' for you?"

Tyray hated Mr. Mitchell's question. What did he know? He wasn't there on the playground years ago when Tyray was an awkward kid people used to tease. He wasn't there last year when Warren was dragged out or when Dad's anger spread like cancer in the house. He wasn't humiliated at school, robbed on the street, or worried if his brother was okay. He never stood in a misty alley holding a gun to his own head. It was all a tangled knot Tyray couldn't unravel, let alone describe to his teacher. And yet, he couldn't shake Mr. Mitchell's question.

"How's that workin' for you?"

Sitting there in the empty classroom,

Tyray knew it *wasn't* working. Not at all. He had no real friends and no one to talk to. The sad truth came crashing down on him in heavy waves. Tyray couldn't stand it.

"Yo, I'm sorry," Tyray said, trying to mask the pain with a smile. "Maybe you helped Darrell with what you're saying, but that don't work on me. I ain't like him, okay? Just 'cause you came to my house don't mean nothin'. No disrespect, but you don't know jack about me, Mr. Mitchell," Tyray said, clenching his jaw to hide his emotion. Sadness filled his chest until it felt as if it would burst. *"No one does,"* he almost added.

Overhead, the bell rang and students lined up in the hallway outside the classroom. Tyray took a deep breath and turned away just as Mr. Mitchell handed him a hall pass. It was already filled out with his name and his next class.

"I might know a bit more than you realize," Mr. Mitchell said. "Remember, you got choices. You hear me? It doesn't have to be this way, Tyray. It can change."

Tyray crumpled the pass and stormed out, his eyes stinging as he left.

*   *   *

After school, Tyray sat in his empty living room. Mr. Mitchell's words kept replaying in his mind.

You have choices.

Tyray didn't see any. Trying to escape his thoughts, he grabbed the remote and flipped on the TV.

Two men fought each other in a cage, kicking and punching as a crowd roared. He pressed the remote.

Click.

A grainy image showed a bomb crash through the chimney of a building. An instant later the structure became a fireball.

Click.

Two women on a talk show were screaming at each other. Suddenly, one stood up, cursed the other, and slapped her face. The audience hooted and cheered.

Tyray switched off the TV, his broken wrist tingling. He wished he could escape the house, just as Lark said. But there was no way out.

He heard the rumble of Dad's truck outside. Quickly, he retreated to his room as the front door unlocked. Tyray heard the familiar slap of his father's keys on the table.

"Tyray!" he called. "You here?"

"Yeah," he hollered back.

"C'mere," Dad said. "I want to talk to you about something."

Tyray felt his pulse quicken. *What if Dad found out that Mom had given him papers to visit Warren? What if Mr. Mitchell called and told him about his falling grades?* He braced himself as he walked into the hallway.

"Why didn't you tell me about this?" His father was holding a piece of paper. It was Tyray's half-completed application from Phat Burger. He had dropped it when he and Dad fought.

Tyray shrugged. "You never gave me a chance," he replied.

His father stared at the paper, as if the words stung him somehow. "You serious about working? It's the first time I ever heard you say you wanted a job."

"Yeah, I'm serious. I gotta pay back Mom, remember?" he replied. He didn't want Dad to know about Lark. "But it don't matter. They ain't gonna hire me."

"Why not?"

He explained what Selma said to him about his broken wrist.

96

"Well, Selma don't know what she's talking about."

"Huh?"

"I know the owner over there. Known him for years. Sometimes my crew goes there for lunch. Anyway, your mother and I talked last night, and I called him today. He said he could use help weekends. You wanna work, you be there at 9:30 next Saturday for training," Dad said.

"For real?" Tyray couldn't believe his father's words.

"Yeah," Dad nodded. "But you're still grounded. This is for work only—and just on Saturdays. Y'hear? If I see any nonsense from you or your grades slip, we gonna drop this real quick. Understand?"

"Don't worry," Tyray replied, glancing down at his cast.

Chapter 8

"Ouch!" Tyray yelled. Droplets of hot grease from the fryer at Phat Burger splattered on his wrist, sending needles of pain into his arm.

"That's the third time today," said Dominic, the nineteen-year-old shift manager who had trained him since he showed up at 9:30. "Here," he said throwing him a towel.

Tyray wiped the grease from his arm and noticed the tiny spots it left on his cast.

"It's 'cause you rush too much. Like I said this morning, you gotta slow down so you don't splash—unless you want your arm to be as cooked as them fries."

"Man, you try doin' this one-handed!" Tyray said, tossing the towel next to the sink. The truth was he had trouble paying attention because his mind was on tomorrow. He still hadn't figured out how he would get Dad to let him go to Cliffside.

"Hey, I told you to stay on the register, but you asked to work back here. Don't go makin' excuses. You're lucky you even got a job," Dominic said.

"*If I was lucky, my wrist wouldn't be broke*," Tyray wanted to say, but he knew to keep his mouth shut. There was no way he would admit he chose to work at the fryer so he wouldn't have to face people from Bluford. Seeing them from the fryer was bad enough.

"How'd you break your wrist again?"

"I told you. I slipped in the cafeteria at school," Tyray said, careful to hide details about Darrell.

"That's not what I heard," said a voice behind him.

Tyray turned to see Selma.

She had barely said a word to him the whole morning.

"Why, what'd you hear?" Dominic asked.

"Yeah, tell us," said Nitza, another girl who worked at the registers.

"Oh my God, I can't believe it," cut in a voice from behind him. Tyray turned

99

around to see Shanetta Green and Natalie Wallace, two older girls he recognized from Bluford. "Tyray Hobbs is flippin' burgers!"

"Look at him!" Shanetta howled, snapping a picture with her camera phone. "Yo, Tyray. That cast come with fries?" she teased.

"Yeah, Ty. Do they sell that cast supersize?" joked Natalie.

The two girls cackled so loudly other customers stared at them. Tyray wanted to tell them off, but he knew he couldn't. He glanced at Lark's writing to stay calm.

"Not so fun when they dishin' it out at *you*, is it?" Selma said with a knowing smile.

Tyray grunted and returned to the fryer, removing the cooked fries from the grease and draining them in a tray before sprinkling salt on them, like Dominic showed him. For a second, he imagined spitting into Shanetta's fries or dumping a bucket of grease on her lap. Finally, the noisy girls grabbed their food and sat down.

"So what did you hear, Selma?" Nitza asked after they left.

Dominic turned his head to listen, even as he rang up a customer's order.

Tyray braced himself. He expected the rest of the crew to laugh at him when she told the truth, but instead Selma gave Tyray a quick glance.

"Nah, I was just playin'. I don't know nothin' about it," she said.

"Girl, why you always playin'?" Nitza complained, as if she was disappointed. Selma changed the subject and walked back to her register.

But later, just as his shift ended, she walked by and whispered, "You owe me."

"Owe you for what?" he asked.

"Not telling on you," she said with a grin. "I heard about how you broke your hand. But I figure since you workin' here now, maybe if I kept quiet, you could cover a shift for me one day. I hate workin' on Sundays."

Tyray's eyes widened. Maybe one day he would cover her shift, but he had something to do first. And she had just given him an idea how to do it.

He almost hugged Selma right there as the plan formed in his head.

A way to get to Cliffside.

"You sure they need you tomorrow?" Dad asked. "An extra day so soon?"

Tyray stretched the truth. It was

dangerous, but he had no choice.

"Yeah. This girl Selma called out, so they're short-staffed tomorrow. You can call Dominic and ask him if you want to," Tyray explained.

Dad studied him for a few seconds. Mom said nothing, but Tyray felt her watching him.

"I told him I was grounded, but he wanted me to ask just in case."

"What did I tell you about working? Saturdays only. Remember?" Dad grumbled.

Tyray knew what to do next.

"You know what, Dad? Forget it. I knew you were gonna say this. I'll just call and cancel." He grabbed the phone pretending to call Dominic. Just then Mom's voice cut in.

"C'mon, Gil," she said. "If they need help, and he wants to work, why not let him? It's only gonna be for a few hours."

"See? There you go again, contradicting me. It ain't no wonder he don't listen."

"But it's *work*, Gil. How many times have you worked late 'cause someone called out? Besides he could be doin' a lot worse than working a few extra hours."

His father rubbed his temples. "Fine! But you be back here by 6:00," Dad growled. "And if I find out you were somewhere outside that burger joint, you're gonna be in the worst trouble of your life. I ain't playin' with you. You hear me?"

Tyray struggled to hide his excitement. He almost wanted to thank his mother for taking his side. He wondered if she knew what he planned to do.

The next morning as he was heading out the door, Mom stopped him.

"Here," she whispered, making sure Dad couldn't see her. She pressed a twenty dollar bill and a small envelope into his hand. Warren's name was written on it.

Tyray realized she knew exactly where he was going, and that she had lied to help him get out. He wished she could join him, that there was no need to lie, no angry divide that cut through their house. For an instant, he almost yelled out in frustration, but she squeezed his arm and quickly turned away.

Tyray raced out the door, carrying the money and the papers inside his sweatshirt. He headed down the block as if he was going to Phat Burger, glancing back until he was sure his father wasn't watching him.

Bones was waiting near where he had sold Tyray the gun weeks earlier. He wore faded black jeans and a ragged T-shirt beneath a denim jacket that hung loose from his thin shoulders. He sipped coffee from a small paper cup cradled in his veiny hands. For a second, he reminded Tyray of one of the homeless people who lived beneath the highway overpass not far away.

"Right on time, boy. Let's do this," Bones said with a crackling voice. He began walking and Tyray was surprised at how quickly the skinny man moved, weaving between cars and crossing busy streets as if he didn't care what happened to him.

"Ain't every day someone like me tries to get back *into* a prison," Bones grumbled, fighting off a cough as they reached the bus stop across from SuperFoods.

The bus stop was a plexiglass shell scribbled with magic marker. On one side, a black and silver movie poster announced that *Moonlight* was coming to theaters soon. Tyray remembered what Lark said and shook his head.

Inside, on the metal bench, sat a woman with braided hair and a small boy who looked to be in preschool. She watched him and Bones warily.

"C'mere, Tevan," she said, yanking the child closer to her.

Tyray imagined what they must look like together when he noticed the boy's eyes locked on his cast.

"Stop starin'! That ain't nice," the woman scolded.

Bones smiled, his teeth crooked and yellow in the morning light.

"Wassup, little man?" he said, putting a hand out so the boy could hit it. "C'mon, give me some," he urged. The little boy slapped it, and Bones chuckled with delight. "That's what I'm talkin' 'bout!" he said before his voice broke into a violent cough.

The boy jumped back into the woman's arms as Bones fought to control himself. Tyray stepped away and scanned the street, hoping the bus would arrive soon. Instead, in the distance, he spotted two people heading toward SuperFoods. One of them was Harold Davis from his English class. He recognized his bulging frame two blocks away. Next to him was Cindy Gibson, another freshman at

Bluford. Tyray couldn't believe they were out together, but just then something else caught his eye.

A gold Nissan with chrome wheels and a slate-tinted windshield.

It whipped by and cut into the grocery store lot. As soon as the car stopped, Londell got out and headed inside. Jupiter and Keenan stepped out but didn't go in the store.

Tyray clenched his fists. What were they doing? Why were they always hanging out so close to his block? He pictured Londell's cold smirk and felt an urge to rush over to his car. So what if he got beat up? At least he would get his chance to hit back. That's more than what anybody else did about them. *Cowards and animals,* he thought to himself. *I don't want to be neither.*

"C'mon," Bones interrupted. His eyes were on the Nissan, too. "Let's go."

Tyray heard the rumble of a bus approaching. The woman next to him stood up and guided Tevan forward.

Within seconds, the bus hissed to a stop in front of them. Tyray stepped inside and grabbed a seat where he could watch the lot. Bones sat right in front of him as the engine groaned and the bus lurched forward. Through the glass, the golden Nissan sparkled like a piece of fake jewelry.

"Twenty years ago, that was me," Bones said, pointing at the sedan. "The OG, ol' school. I had so much swagger you couldn't fit me in that car. Londell's father was the same way. We grew up in the projects together. We had each other's back for a time, but that ain't enough out here," he scoffed. "See what respect on the street gets you? You either end up dead, in jail, or alone. Me, I've had two out of three, and the third is comin' quick. As for Julius James, he's already gone. His kids are following the same path. But you . . . maybe not."

Tyray turned from the window and looked at the skinny man. He couldn't help but notice the cordlike veins in his wiry neck, the papery skin that covered his face. He realized he was staring at Bones the way Tevan had stared at his cast.

"Time's always goin' forward on us. We can't never go back and undo what we did. If we could, man, the things I'd change . . ."

Bones's voice cracked, and he turned away as the streets faded into a blur.

*　*　*

Nearly two hours later, Tyray spotted the exit sign for Cliffside Correctional Facility. Bones had guided Tyray through two bus transfers but otherwise ignored him.

Tyray's legs were stiff as he stepped off the bus and faced a massive stone wall the color of dirty cardboard. On top stretched an endless coil of silvery wire studded with toothlike barbs. Tyray cringed thinking of Warren trapped behind it.

"This way," Bones said, leading him to a steel door with a wired-glass window. A sign above it read "Visitor Entrance." A small crowd followed them, including Tevan and his mother. The boy looked exhausted.

"Where's Daddy?" he whined, tugging at her arm. "I want Daddy."

Behind her stood an older woman, her hair mostly gray and her back hunched as if she was carrying some invisible weight.

"Get in line," Bones directed. "I'll stay with you until they let you through."

"You ain't goin' inside?" Tyray asked.

"No, this is your visit, not mine,"

Bones replied. "Besides, he don't wanna see me right now. But tell him what I said, and tell him I brought you here too. That's gotta count for somethin'."

They joined the line of visitors that led to an imposing steel counter as tall as Tyray's chest. Behind it were several uniformed officers, their faces stern and serious. When Tyray got to the front, an officer asked him for his paperwork and ID. He handed over everything Mom had given him. The officer studied the papers carefully.

"Warren Hobbs didn't indicate to us that a visitor was coming today," the guard said. "You're supposed to have a parent with you, too."

"His parents couldn't be here today," Bones chimed in. "I'm an old friend of the family just bringin' the boy to see his brother. They ain't seen each other in a year."

The prison guard eyed Bones and Tyray warily. "No one told us about any of this."

"Please. He's my brother. It's my first time here," Tyray urged. He couldn't hide the desperation in his voice. "I wanted to surprise him."

"Yeah, well we don't do surprises

here," the officer barked. "We're gonna have to check with him. Go have a seat and we'll call you."

Tyray sat on an uncomfortable bench and watched as Tevan and his mother were sent through a metal detector. The boy cried out as the officers forced him to walk separately from his mother.

"It's okay, baby," she said over and over again.

But it wasn't okay, Tyray thought to himself. No child should have to be in such a place. Next to him, Bones shook his head grimly as if he shared his thoughts.

"Tyray Hobbs," called out the guard nearly a half hour later. "Step this way."

Tyray walked over to the metal detector and a guard directed him through. Then another guard wearing white rubber gloves patted his chest, armpits, legs, and backside. Tyray felt strange with the man's hands all over his body.

"You got anything in there?" the guard asked, pointing to his cast.

"Just my broken hand," Tyray answered.

The officer glared for a second and waved a small metal detector over his cast. Then Tyray was led down a dull cement corridor that smelled of bleach and paint. Video cameras were mounted overhead at each end. The corridor ended with a massive steel door positioned next to a glass room where two guards sat watching TV monitors. The guard next to Tyray pulled out a key and inserted it into the door.

CLUNK

Tyray flinched as the heavy lock clicked and the door opened with an ominous metallic groan. Inside was a bare room with simple tables. At one sat a man wearing an orange jumpsuit with the words "Cliffside Correctional Facility." He held Tevan in his arms. The woman with braided hair stood at the man's side, her hands on his back, and whispered in his ear.

In the far corner was another table with a broad-shouldered man whose head was almost completely shaved. His neck was ripped with muscle, and he wore the same jumpsuit. Only his eyes looked just like Mom's.

It was Warren.

Chapter 9

"Whatchu doin' here, T?!" Warren shouted, his voice a mix of surprise and concern. "What happened to your hand?"

Tyray couldn't answer. Waves of emotion crashed through his chest. The humiliation he faced at Bluford, the loneliness he felt at home, the worry since he spoke to Londell, the sadness that overtook him in the dark alley, the relief of seeing Warren's face. It overwhelmed him, making it impossible to speak. He crossed the room in silence and embraced his brother.

"It's okay, bro," Warren said, slapping his back several times. "It's okay."

"Man, why'd you stop writing to me? Huh?" Tyray asked, his head buried in his brother's chest, his eyes stinging with tears. "I was scared . . ."

"I'm sorry," Warren said gently, letting him go. His face was fuller than Tyray remembered, and he looked older. A jagged scar extended just above his right eyebrow. It had once been a deep gash, Tyray could see, but the wound was mostly healed now.

"You okay?" Tyray asked, eyeing the scar. "What happened?"

"Nothin'," Warren said, shaking his head as if the topic annoyed him. "Just a scratch, that's all. Dad send you to check up on me?"

"No! He don't even know I'm here," Tyray admitted, explaining how he snuck out to the prison to visit him.

"Why'd you do that? You know he's gonna find out, and then it's gonna be trouble for you."

"It can't get much worse," Tyray grumbled. "You still didn't answer me. How come you never wrote back?"

Warren shook his head wearily. "Look, it wasn't about you, okay? I know Mom and Dad read what I write you. And I'm tired of lying to everybody. That's what got me into this mess, and I can't do it no more. If people can't handle the truth, then I got nothing to say to 'em, not even Mom and especially not Dad. I

113

got no time for him."

"Whatchu mean? I never asked you to lie about nothin'."

"Look, T, just drop it, all right? Tell me what's going on at home. And school. Give me something else to think about besides this place."

"No. You can't shut me out like that. I been worried about you and thinkin' the worst. I see that scar on your face. What's goin' on? For real, what's up?"

Warren rubbed his head and sighed heavily. "You ain't a kid no more, so I guess I can tell you. But this just between you and me, y'hear?"

Tyray nodded, staring into his brother's unblinking eyes.

"I'm a father."

"*What?*" Tyray felt as if the world suddenly shifted and pitched forward.

"Me and Chantel. Remember?"

Tyray recalled the visitor list and Mom's old complaints about Warren spending too much time with her. It made sense, and yet it felt wrong, too. Tyray remembered Warren doing home-work at the kitchen table or playing X-box in front of the TV before Dad came home. He couldn't imagine him being a parent. Other people had kids, but not his brother. Not now. Not like this.

"You serious?"

Warren nodded. "When I found out she was pregnant, I freaked. There ain't no way I was gonna tell Dad. I was still in school. I was supposed to be looking at colleges. How was I gonna take care of a kid? So I started thinking about getting money. That's when I did the dumbest thing of my life. I listened to this dude Bones and hit that store," he whispered.

The room seemed to lurch again. *Bones gave you the idea?* Tyray felt as if the top of his head was about to explode.

"You're the only one in our family that knows this, T. Check this out." Warren held out a tiny worn photograph smaller than his old iPod. A smiling baby girl with tiny pink beads in her hair looked out from it. She had Warren's eyes.

"That's Jayda. Your niece. She's almost a year old now. She's why I lift weights, why I read books, why I got my GED. I'm hoping to do right for her once I get outta here. I got two years left."

Two years. A niece. Tyray took a deep breath.

"Visiting hours end in thirty minutes," a guard announced.

"I know Dad can't handle it. If I have

to hear another lecture on responsibility, I'ma scream. Yeah, I messed up, but I'm trying to make it right. I'm a tutor in here, Tyray. Some guys don't even know how to read, and I'm teaching 'em. They call me Prof 'cause I'm their professor. If I keep it up, I might get out six months early for good behavior. So I'm tryin'. It ain't perfect, but it's all I got right now besides her." He looked at the tiny picture in his hands. "Sorry I hid all this for so long, but you understand, right?"

Tyray nodded, dizzy with what he had learned. It all made sense. Warren's secrecy. His fight with Dad. Bones's apology. The skinny man had led Warren into trouble. Maybe he had sold him his gun, too.

"No wonder Bones said you wouldn't want to see him," he mumbled, anger swelling in his chest.

"*Bones*? Whatchu doin' talkin' to *him*?"

Tyray took a deep breath. There was no reason to lie. "He brought me here."

"What? He's here! *Now*?" Warren hissed. "Boy, are you crazy?"

A guard in the corner of the room craned his neck toward them.

"Is there a problem, Mr. Hobbs?"

116

"No," Warren said, cradling the tiny picture in his hands. "Ain't no problems."

"He's dyin'," Tyray explained. "Told me to tell you he's sorry, but them words ain't good enough, if you ask me."

Warren winced at the words and leaned forward in his chair.

"Man, tell me what's been goin' on with you, T," he said, looking at Tyray's cast. "Tell me everything."

Tyray's head pounded. He knew Warren had no idea what happened at school with Darrell. He wanted to tell him the truth, but he couldn't say the words. *I wanted to shoot myself. Sometimes I still wish I did.* They were locked tight in his throat.

Instead Tyray told the version he had told his parents, careful to keep his voice low when he mentioned the gun and Bones. Then he explained what Londell said and what made him rush to Cliffside.

Warren clenched his teeth and shook his head as if what he heard pained him.

"Boy, are you trying to end up in here? 'Cause that's what's gonna happen if you keep this up. And believe me, you don't want to be in this place. There are things that happen in here . . . I can't even talk about it," Warren's voice broke up. "I wish I was out there to help you, bro. But you gotta listen to me. I don't care what Bones says. Stay away from him. Maybe I'd never be here if it weren't for him. I don't know. As for Londell, he's dangerous. He gave me this," Warren said, pointing to the scar over his eye.

"*What!?*" Tyray couldn't believe it. So it was true. Londell hadn't lied.

"He was here and saw me teachin' people. Said I was wasting my time. When I told him about Jayda, he said the only way I could afford to raise her was to work for him. I guess I acted like Dad then," Warren admitted, smiling bitterly. "I couldn't take it. My baby girl deserves better than a daddy who served time and sells drugs for Londell James. I lost it and shoved him. Another mistake. Good thing a few guys got my back or it woulda been even worse for me. You stay away from him. Dude's father was murdered a few years ago. He's scary. You cross him, and he'll take you down in a heartbeat."

"His brother robbed me twice," Tyray grumbled, remembering his fight with Jupiter and how Londell had threatened him. "They're hangin' all the time near Union Street. I seen 'em out there this morning—"

"Ten minutes," announced the guard, cutting Tyray off.

Warren leaned forward, his hands near his chest as if he was about to pass an invisible basketball.

"Listen, T. I'ma break this down for you quick. You're an endangered species. Comin' from our neighborhood, we got a better chance endin' up in jail than goin' to college. An old iPod don't matter. Forty bucks ain't nothin'. Whoever thinks that stuff is important ain't spent time in here! A week behind bars, and they'd trade it all back to be on the outside again, you understand?"

Tyray nodded as Warren continued.

"Get your education. Build yourself up so you never have to see a place like this. Be the one who invents the next iPod, not the one who spends all your money on it. And if you can't do it for yourself, do it for your niece who don't have her daddy 'cause he messed up when he was standing where you are right now. Or do it for me, your brother who's failing his family 'cause he's locked up in the joint."

Warren's voice shook with sadness, anger, and regret. Tyray knew those

119

feelings. They reminded him of his night in the alley.

"You ain't failing," Tyray said, trying to think of something to comfort him. "You helpin' me, right?"

Just then Tyray realized he wanted to tell his brother everything that happened with Darrell. He knew, looking in Warren's eyes, that his brother would listen and maybe even understand. But before he could say another word, the guard approached.

"Time to wrap it up, everyone," he announced. Tevan cried out in the distance.

"Listen to me, T. You still got a chance. You're still in school. Promise me you're gonna make it count," Warren urged, his eyes almost desperate.

Promise. The word struck Tyray. The same word Lark used. The same one emblazoned on his cast. For a second, he couldn't speak.

"That's it. Let's move," the guard barked, tapping Warren on the shoulder.

Warren stood up, and Tyray hugged him again. For several seconds it was quiet, and Tyray wished he could just bring his brother home with him. But instead, he had to let him go. He handed him Mom's letter and watched as the guards led him away.

"I miss you, bro," Warren added as he turned down the corridor.

"Me too," Tyray said, watching him disappear behind a heavy steel door. "Me too."

Tyray confronted Bones on the bus home.

"So you sold a gun to my brother and told him to go rob a store?"

Bones nodded. "I told you I was sorry," he said, looking skinnier than ever.

"He's a father now and can't raise his baby girl 'cause of you," Tyray fumed.

Bones shrugged his shoulders wearily. "He ain't the only one not coming home 'cause of me," he said, almost in a whisper.

Tyray wanted to hit him. He pictured his fist slamming into the frail man's bony face. As sick as he was, Bones would be no match for him. And yet the thought made Tyray feel dirty inside.

"Man, I don't wanna talk to you again. Just stay away from me, okay?"

Bones nodded, his eyes bloodshot and glassy. He was silent the entire ride home.

* * *

Sunday night, Tyray stared at the ceiling of his bedroom, the news of the day swirling like a storm in his head. He still couldn't believe what he had learned.

Warren was a father.

He was an uncle.

His parents didn't know.

Tyray felt as if he were lying to their faces each time he saw them. And yet he was angry, too. Maybe if Dad weren't so strict, Warren could have told them the truth. Maybe he wouldn't have felt so desperate and done something so stupid. Maybe he never would have ended up in jail.

Tyray knew he was the same way. Alone and desperate. That's what led him to make his mistakes, too. Seeing Bones. Stealing money. Getting a gun.

"How's that workin' for you?" Mr. Mitchell's question mocked him. He knew the answer just as Warren knew it as he sat month after month in prison. It wasn't working. Not at all.

Knock. Knock.

The sound against the door startled him.

"You awake?"

It was Mom's voice. Tyray got up and opened the door. He peered back into the living room and saw Dad asleep on the couch. His mother stepped into the room and gently closed the door.

"So did you go? Did you see him?" she asked.

The question irritated him. It was another secret he was supposed to keep. Another moment where he couldn't tell the truth. He was getting sick of it.

"Yeah, I saw him," he said, sitting down on his mattress and crossing his arms. The bitterness he felt inside was spreading like a rash.

"Well? How is he?"

"He's locked up, Mom. What do you want me to say?" Tyray grumbled, careful to keep his promise to Warren.

His mother stepped closer. "That's it? Did you talk to him about the argument with your father, and why he won't see us?"

"We didn't have a lot of time, Mom," Tyray replied, hating that he had to lie. "He's working. Teaching people to read and stuff. And he looked good, like he's been hittin' the weights."

His mother looked confused, as if she had expected something else, something more. "Well, what'd he say to you? Why hasn't he written back?" she demanded, her voice rising in frustration.

"You and Dad shouldn'tve pushed him away. If you didn't, maybe it wouldn't be this way."

"What way? What did he tell you?"

You're a grandma now, Mom. The words were on the tip of his tongue, but like so many others, he couldn't say them.

"You should go visit him," he replied. "Ask him yourself, okay? I don't wanna be in the middle," Tyray blurted. He turned away from her and stared at his wall. He could see Lark's writing on his cast and wanted to scratch it off.

"Tyray, are you okay? Did he say something that upset you?" Mom asked.

"Just talk to him, Mom. No matter what Dad says."

He kept his back to her and listened as she walked out and shut the door.

In the quiet darkness, he recalled what his brother had told him. Warren's final words echoed like a sad song in his mind, one he could not shake.

"You're an endangered species . . . Get your education . . . Do it for me."

Mr. Mitchell had practically said the same thing. In his own way, Bones said

124

it, too. Could they all be wrong?

They acted as if it was so simple, as if he could just flip a switch and all his problems would go away, and he would suddenly be a perfect student. Who were they kidding? If it were so easy, why was Bones on the street? Why was Warren in jail?

He felt his cast in the dark. Inside, he was supposed to be healing, and yet everything outside felt as if it was coming apart. Still, Warren's words stuck with him.

"You're still in school. Promise me you're gonna make it count."

Hours later, still unable to sleep, Tyray turned on his light, grabbed his copy of *Lord of the Flies*, and flipped it open.

Chapter 10

Tyray didn't talk to Mr. Mitchell or anyone in his class about what he had been doing. But each day after school, he retreated to his room and read.

At first he was bored with the book and its weird, old-fashioned words, but then he started to wonder what was going to happen to the kids stranded on the island. Some were as young as Tevan, not much older than his niece.

Tyray even stayed up late one night reading. The story grew bloodier and more violent. He shuddered when Piggy—the kid Tasha said reminded her of Harold—is killed by his classmates.

"That ain't right," he whispered in the dark.

But as he read, he knew in some ways, it was just like the cafeteria during

126

his fight, like the neighborhood when Jupiter jumped him, like some of his own treatment of Harold and Darrell.

No wonder Mr. Mitchell assigned it, Tyray figured.

At one point, Tyray had to put the book down because it bothered him so much. It was a scene where a group of boys slaughter a pig. The writer describes the spears sinking into its body, the blood spurting on the boys' hands, all of them chanting as the dying animal squeals. Some of the boys seemed to have violence in their hearts. Others were so scared that they joined in, even though they knew it was wrong.

Cowards and animals, Tyray thought, *just like I said.* Maybe that's how most people were, but Tyray knew he didn't want to be like that, no matter what he had done in the past or what classmates like Jamee thought about him.

Tyray even wrote about it on the final test for the book two weeks later. When Mr. Mitchell reviewed the exam, he read aloud some of Tyray's answer. People stared as if he was from another planet, as if they couldn't believe Tyray Hobbs knew how to read or write—or think.

Who needs any of y'all, Tyray thought,

trying to hold on to what his brother said, though he felt almost invisible at Bluford and at home.

"Get your education . . . Do it for me."

But on Friday at lunch a week later, he could see that something was wrong with Lark. She didn't smile or speak when she sat next to him. Instead, she grunted, her eyes locked in another thick vampire book as if the cover could somehow shield her from the real world. She didn't even touch her lunch.

"Girl, what's your problem? You ain't said a word to me yet. You okay?" he asked.

Even her friends seem concerned, eyeing her from their lunch table more than usual.

"I just don't feel like talking about it, okay?" she said, flipping a page and not bothering to look at him.

"Now you sound like me," Tyray mumbled. "But *you* always make *me* talk."

Lark sighed and lowered the book from her face. Her eyes were puffy and bloodshot, as if she had been crying. Her sweatshirt was wrinkled, and cat fur was sprinkled across it as if it hadn't been washed in days.

"Please, can you just drop it?"

He had never seen her so serious. The scar above her lip was stretched thin and taut, as if it were about to snap.

"But you can tell Jamee and not me?" Tyray said, unable to hide his frustration.

She shrugged, avoiding his gaze.

"You know what? Fine. Don't tell me. I don't even want to know." He stood up from the table with his tray. It pained him to say the words, but she was shutting him out as if it didn't matter that he cared about her, though he had never admitted it.

"Wait," she said, putting her book down. "Where you goin'?"

"Well, since you got nothin' to say to me, what am I gonna say to you?" he huffed, angry at himself for snapping at her. He started to walk away.

"Tyray. Please don't go. Don't leave me here alone."

He turned back. She seemed broken somehow. He knew her friends were watching, but they didn't matter. What struck him was the sadness in her voice. There was no way he would walk away from her now.

"What is it? You can talk to me."

"It's my brother, Kyle," she said.

"Your brother?"

"He's only in seventh grade, but these older boys in our neighborhood are always tryin' to get him to hang out. I know they're no good. I keep tryin' to tell him, but he don't wanna listen to me. My mom's always workin' nights. And my dad . . . just forget him. I'm the only one who knows," she said, her eyes starting to glaze.

"Knows what?"

"They're sellin', okay? Everyone on our street's scared, especially since the older one just got out of jail. I fought with Kyle for hours last night, but he just ignores me. Says I don't understand. I found a gun in his room, Tyray. What am I supposed to do? He's my little brother."

Her description snagged in Tyray's mind like skin on a rusty nail. His stomach began to sink. He knew the answer to his question before he asked it.

"Where do you live?"

"The corner of 43rd Street," Lark said. "Why you asking me that?"

Tyray lowered his head and cursed. That was Londell's neighborhood.

The roar of the busy cafeteria suddenly seemed choked and muffled. The crowd all around him became dim and transparent. In that instant, Bluford itself seemed to fall away. In its place were the details of Lark's description. They came together in Tyray's mind like some horrible puzzle. Before she could say any more, Tyray knew exactly who was after Lark's brother.

The same crew that robbed him twice.

The same ones Bones had warned him about.

The one who left a scar on his brother's face.

"One of them drive a gold Nissan?" he asked, just to be sure.

"Yeah. How'd you know that?"

Boom!

Tyray pounded his fist on the lunch table. The impact cracked like a gunshot in the cafeteria. Heads turned in alarm.

"Tyray, why'd you do that?! What's wrong?"

"I know the guy your brother's messin' with," Tyray replied grimly.

"How?"

"It's a long story," he grumbled, the danger of Kyle's situation sinking in with each passing second.

"I'm scared, Tyray," Lark admitted.

131

She stared down at her book as if she was searching for a way out. "I know they're dangerous. Thing is, I know Kyle's scared, too. That's the worst part. I can see it in his eyes. He's still just a kid, you know. It shouldn't be like this."

Tyray cursed under his breath. He couldn't stand the pain and worry in Lark's voice, and the thought that it was all happening again.

Another family being pulled apart.

Another gun ready to ruin a life.

Another kid out of control, spinning toward jail. Or worse.

Tyray knew it all too well. He had been there and was still fighting it every day. The wounds were in his bones, the scars on his face and in his heart.

We're an endangered species, just like Warren said, he thought.

He hated how true it was and how weak and powerless he felt. And yet something began to gnaw at him, a spark of an idea that flared into a flame deep in his chest. Something he never would have considered before his experience in the alley with Darrell. He turned and grabbed Lark's hand.

"I'll talk to Kyle," he said suddenly. "Tomorrow night after work."

"For real? You'd do that?" Lark asked. Her face lit up as if he had suddenly given her a lifeline, but then it clouded over just as quickly. "Wait. You gotta be careful. You don't wanna get in the middle of this."

"Relax, girl," he said, hiding his own worries. He knew what it was like to cross Londell, and so did Warren. But he couldn't tell Lark that, or she would never let him go. "It's just a little talk, that's all. Ain't no big thing."

"But Tyray—"

"It's all right," he said, feeling his broken hand tingle nervously in his cast. "I got this."

Tyray arrived almost an hour early at Phat Burger on Saturday morning, hoping maybe he could leave before it got dark, but Dominic refused.

"Sorry, T, but I need you until 6:00. It's Saturday, remember?"

Tyray nodded grimly. He had spent most of last night staring at the ceiling, wondering what he could say to Kyle. What worried him most was Londell finding out what he was doing. If what he planned to do worked, Tyray knew that Londell would find out tonight.

Then things would probably get ugly.

"It's payday!" Selma announced as Tyray tossed a fresh batch of French fries into a pool of hot, bubbling grease, the splatters dotting his cast. "Whatchu got planned for this weekend?"

"Nothin'," he lied. He knew where his money was going. He had been waiting for this first paycheck since he started two weeks ago. Beyond that, Tyray had no idea. Londell and Jupiter stalked his thoughts. He knew they would be in his future again. Soon.

"I'ma see that new *Moonlight* movie," Selma added as if she didn't care whether anyone listened. "It's gonna be da bomb."

"It's playin' tonight?" he asked, remembering how Lark wanted to see it.

"Duh! Where you been? That's, like, what everyone's talkin' about," she said.

Tyray shrugged. He didn't care about the stupid movie, and yet something about it pained him. He couldn't remember the last time he had gone to the movies. That was something others did, people with friends. Classmates who laughed in school and whose families were whole. He hadn't felt that way in years. Maybe never.

You know Londell's gonna come for you if you do this, Tyray thought.

The truth haunted him all day, whispered to him between customers, mocked him as the hours melted away.

"Yo, you all right? You look sick or somethin'," said Dominic at one point, breaking his thoughts.

"I'm fine," Tyray answered, trying to hide the worry that grew by the second. "Be better once I get paid."

"I heard that!" Selma said with a smile.

At 6:00, Tyray yanked off his visor and waited as Dominic slowly cashed out everyone's paychecks. He received an envelope with $97.19. He shoved the money deep into his pocket, feeling his stomach sink as he glanced out the drive-thru window. The sun was already sinking low in the sky.

He had to go. Now.

Chapter 11

Tyray stormed through the crowded restaurant, darting through the greasy air and the rows of tables as he moved toward the door. He had almost reached it when he heard a familiar wheeze.

He looked up to see Bones at the last table near the door. A silvery burger wrapper slathered with ketchup rested in front of him. Bits of fries and a sliver of roll were all that remained of his meal. For a second, their eyes met.

Man, not now, Tyray thought to himself, rushing to the door.

He had to stop and wait as a woman and two kids walked in. Tyray could barely keep still as the kids struggled with the heavy door. He could feel Bones examining him. Instinctively he felt the money in his pocket, and then bolted out the door.

Outside, the sun hung just above the horizon like an angry red eyeball. Long shadows stretched across the sidewalk, and the streets were bathed in a bloody glow.

Tyray hurried. Cars thundered past. Some throbbed with a thumping bass that rattled windows and shook the pit of his stomach, but he didn't care.

Lark was the only one who stood by him in Bluford, the only one who had trusted him and his promise, the only one who stopped each day at school from being an unending desert. Now she needed his help. He had to get Kyle away from Londell, no matter what, even if it would make him a target.

Tyray turned off Union Street. He glanced at his cast. He could still see the words Lark wrote, though they were faded and stained in the dying sunlight.

T's promise.

"That's right," he mumbled to himself, walking past a house with a busted fence and graffiti scrawled on the front wall. Somewhere behind him a dog barked, and another wheezed and growled in the distance, but Tyray kept walking.

Though it was only six blocks from Phat Burger, the neighborhood was very different. Everyone at Bluford knew that 43rd Street was rough. Sure, there were some old people and a few families, but at night they weren't out. Instead, once the sun went down, they hid inside small single-story homes with iron bars on their windows and their doors shut and locked. After dark, the area was a place where no one went unless they were looking for something they shouldn't have. Tyray had gone there the first time he wanted to buy a gun. He had no idea that was where Lark lived.

Tyray reached 43rd Street and began looking for Lark's house. She had said she lived on a corner, but which one? He scanned each. At the last one stood a tiny gray house, its walls drab and peeling, a trash can sitting on the curb. Inside, the windows glowed yellow against the growing darkness. In one, Tyray spotted a large tan cat. He knew it was the right place.

He walked up to the tiny porch and knocked on the door. Within seconds, he heard footsteps. Then the door opened.

Lark faced him, her eyes swollen and wet from tears.

"What is it? What happened?" he asked.

"It's Kyle. He's over there now. I know he doesn't want to be there, but he's scared. He's afraid to tell them no, but they want him to start runnin' for them. Makin' deliveries. I can't call the police. What am I supposed to do?"

"Where's the gun?"

"I hid it so he couldn't find it. He's so upset. Thinks they're gonna get mad at him and me, but I can't let him have it. He's gonna hurt someone or get himself killed."

Tyray snapped. He couldn't stand to see Lark so upset, and he couldn't bear the thought of Londell hurting a member of her family. First it was his brother. Then him. Now his only friend. It was too much.

"Give it to me," he barked. Maybe it would give him protection, he thought. A chance to take back something from Londell that wasn't his: Lark's brother.

"What?! No, Tyray. I can't do that! I can't have something happen to you."

"I ain't gonna use it. I'm gonna get Kyle back."

"Please, Tyray! Don't go over there. Don't do this. I can't have you getting hurt for me."

"I'm goin' either way, but I got a better chance of coming back if you give it to me. C'mon, girl!" he urged.

Tears streamed from Lark's eyes as she rushed back into her house. Seconds later, she came out holding a black handgun as if it disgusted and frightened her. "What are you gonna do? Promise me you're coming back."

Tyray slipped the gun from her hand and shoved it under the waist of his pants. Then he grabbed the envelope of money from his pocket. "Here you go," he said. "It's everything I took from you and more. It's yours. It's what I promised, remember?"

"Wait. Why do you sound that way? Why you giving all this to me?"

He turned away even as she kept calling his name. He had tried to hide his worry, but the words had given it away. He knew he might not come back. He wanted to pay her just in case.

Tyray crossed 43rd Street and then slowed down, careful not to draw attention to himself. Parked on the curb up ahead was the golden Nissan Tyray had seen so many times. He knew eyes might be watching him as he headed up the block. He didn't have much time.

His heart rattled in his chest. His stomach churned. He knew he was in over his head. He could feel it even as he stepped closer to the house. Like so many times before, the world was slipping out of control again. He knew it and wished he could pull it back, bring it back from the edge, but his feet kept moving. Carrying him closer.

Up ahead, he could see the familiar cracked sidewalk. The stained cement driveway. The small enclosed porch not much different than his own.

Tyray reached down and felt the warm metal of the gun against his palm. His hands tingled as if invisible spiders were crawling on his fingers. He couldn't believe he was back where he had been only a month ago.

He had come so far in that time. He could see it now. He had reconnected with Warren. He got a job. He was even doing a little better in school. But still, it was as if he was stuck in quicksand. A kind of gravity was pulling him down, even though he knew inside that it was wrong and dangerous and stupid.

Maybe if Warren wasn't in jail, maybe if school wasn't full of people who hated him, maybe if Dad's ugly words hadn't echoed in his mind for weeks, maybe then he could stop himself. But not now. A grim momentum carried him forward— the anger at Londell, the outrage of what was happening to Lark, the frustration of what had happened to him for weeks. It drove him.

He crept up the driveway that ran next to the house. Inside lights were on. People were talking. He heard a boy's voice. He was sure it was Kyle.

Tyray paused, took a last deep breath, and pulled out the weapon.

Whap!

A clawlike hand gripped his shoulder.

Tyray jerked free and turned with the gun to see Bones. In the dim light, his face looked shadowy and hollow.

"Man, whatchu doin' here?!" Tyray hissed.

"Been followin' you . . ." Bones wheezed, trying to catch his breath. "Knew you was in trouble. Saw it in your face," he said with a weak, raspy voice. His weary eyes focused on the gun. "Don't do this."

"Man, this ain't about you. Just go home!"

Tyray heard the porch door open behind him. He whipped around with the gun, but Bones grabbed it.

"I wasn't gonna use it. Let go!" Tyray snarled, trying to shake the gun free. But the skinny man clung to the weapon as if his life were at stake. With both arms, he twisted and bent Tyray's hand backward. A burning stab of pain shot into his wrist. With his other hand useless, Tyray had to let go.

"What are you doin'?!" he screamed in outrage.

Bones staggered two steps, stumbled, and then fell to the ground. His chest heaved as he lay on the cement. Londell stood right in front of him. He glanced once at Bones and then glared at Tyray as if the sick man wasn't even there.

"Boy, you're even dumber than your brother," Londell fumed.

The porch door opened again, and Jupiter and Keenan rushed out. Next to them stood a shorter, baby-faced boy with Lark's cheekbones. Tyray knew it was Kyle. He looked as if he was ready to throw up.

"Dang, look at these two. Broken Bones and Skin and Bones," Jupiter said as he stepped into the driveway.

"I warned you last time, but you

didn't listen. Now you're done. We goin' for a ride. Let's go," Londell said.

Bones coughed then, making a horrific gurgling sound. Tyray could hear the fluid in his lungs as he heaved and spit onto the ground. Jupiter stopped for a second and stared at the man.

"Go on, Joop! Throw this punk in the car," Londell ordered.

"No!" Bones gasped, his voice almost a gargle. Amazingly, the man stood up. His mouth hung open as he gasped for air. A thin trail of fluid ran from his lip to his chin. And yet his eyes still burned with a determined fire as he stumbled closer.

Londell stepped back as if he was surprised. Jupiter stood frozen. Kyle's jaw dropped.

"Bones, you like a legend out here. But this ain't about you," Londell said. Tyray could see a cruel glint in his eye. "No disrespect, but I got a score to settle with this punk. You had your time. This is *my* time."

Bones staggered between Tyray and Londell, as if he was trying to shield Tyray.

"Me and your pops were friends . . . had each other's backs for years. You remember, don't you?" Bones spoke

144

barely above a whisper, stopping once to cough and spit.

Londell's eyes narrowed at the mention of his father. Jupiter turned toward Bones then, too.

"Bro, he don't look so good," whispered Keenan to Jupiter.

"He promised me . . . if I needed a favor to call him," Bones continued. "So I'm asking you . . . a last favor to an old friend . . . Tyray and this other boy . . . they with me. Let them go . . ." Bones's eyes locked on Londell's. For an instant, the two stared at each other.

Tyray felt glued to the driveway. He knew his own life hung in the balance. Part of him wanted to strip the gun from Bones's hand. But another part knew better. Bones was struggling to save him and Kyle, two kids he barely knew. It was a heroic gesture Tyray couldn't fully comprehend, even as he listened to each breath rattle in the man's chest.

Suddenly, another violent spasm ripped through Bones's body. He collapsed to his hands and knees. The gun fell to the ground with a heavy clunk. All of them stared at it for an instant.

Keenan turned away as Bones spat up a bloody glob. Jupiter gazed on as if he was witnessing an accident happen in slow motion. Kyle turned away as if he was horrified. Londell grunted and picked up the weapon, but Tyray didn't care. He rushed to Bones's side and kneeled next to him, hoping he could help in some way.

"He needs an ambulance," Tyray pleaded. Bones's hands and legs twitched with each cough as he labored for air. *"Please!"*

Londell watched them for a few seconds and then turned toward his house. The older boys followed him, glancing back at Bones several times. Kyle was motionless, his unblinking eyes now fixed on Bones.

"Don't either of you come back here, or you'll end up like him," Londell said. He glared at Tyray and then at Kyle before walking back inside and shutting the door. Bones lay sprawled on the cement.

An ambulance came ten minutes later, but by then it was too late.

Tyray was still at Bones's side when the flashing lights first sliced the darkness. He had heard the man whisper his last words just before a coughing spell stole his final breath.

"Make it count."

Tyray watched as the paramedics pumped Bones's chest and wheeled him into the back of the ambulance. Kyle sat motionless on the curb nearby, his head between his knees as the doors slammed shut and the vehicle raced away. The small crowd that had been drawn by the flashing lights began to disperse when someone shouted out.

"Tyray! Kyle!"

Tyray turned to see Lark. She ran straight to her brother's side and hugged him. The boy's eyes glistened in the streetlight, and he lowered his head into her shoulder. He looked like a young child in her arms.

"I saw the ambulance and was so worried. Are you both okay?" she asked, looking toward Tyray.

He nodded but couldn't speak. There were no words to describe what he had witnessed, no way to explain the gift that Bones had just given them.

An hour later, Lark's mom drove Tyray back to his house.

Lark sat next to him in the back seat, whispering to him words that he had never heard before, words that gradually pulled him back from the horrors of the night and into the moment with her.

"Thank you. You're the bravest person I ever met. I can't believe what you did for us."

Lark's mother and Kyle had said the same thing, but Lark kept close to him, rubbing his back and holding his hand. Once, she wiped a tear racing down his cheek, and he stared into her face. Her eyes shone with concern and gratitude, respect and appreciation. It was as if he had been trapped on some deserted island, and somehow, after everything, she had now come to rescue him. He couldn't help but notice the mysterious mark where she had been hurt long ago. Despite whatever damage had been done, Lark had remained honest and gentle and true. It was all new to him. Treasures he had never seen before.

"You need to talk to me," she urged at a red light near his house. "I need to know what's going on in there."

"You don't even want to know," he mumbled.

"No, Tyray. I do," she replied, touching the cast where she had written. "Don't you get it? *I do.*"

Tyray closed his eyes and leaned into her. He felt the warmth of her body against his. Hot tears rolled down his face, streams of pain and sorrow that seemed to know no end. He couldn't talk now. It was all too much, too soon. But for the first time in his memory, he realized that he had someone who wanted to hear what he had to say. Someone who trusted and valued him, no matter what anyone else said. It was a new world waiting to be discovered. Thanks to Bones, he would be able to explore it with her. The man had bought him that chance.

But what did that mean? Tyray didn't know. So much was wrong at home with his family. His brother was still in jail, and Londell was still out there. None of that had changed. Yet inside, after everything, he felt different somehow. He had pulled a kid off the streets, at least for now. He had helped a friend and stood up for what was right. The more he thought about it, the more he knew that Dad and Jamee and the others at Bluford were wrong about him. He had made mistakes, but he was a good person, too.

Because of Bones, he had avoided prison and death. He had also reconnected with Warren, something he knew he would do again. Maybe every Sunday from now on. And he had fulfilled his promise to Lark. Now what would happen with her? He had no idea. For an instant, he pictured them together at the movies seeing *Moonlight* as if they were just like anybody else. A normal couple. It was silly, but it made him grateful for the possibilities. Paths once invisible suddenly opened to him. Tyray could see them now. Bones had shown him that.

"Make it count," Bones had said.

"I will," Tyray answered him.

It was a kind of promise, he realized, one he knew he had to keep.

The next day, after a late-night talk that left his parents in stunned silence, Tyray Hobbs took the long ride back to Cliffside Prison. Only this time, he was in the back seat of his parents' car. They had decided to join him. Tyray couldn't believe it.

Dad's jaw was tight, and Mom looked nervous as they got in the car together. There was still so much that needed to be said. Tyray could feel it like an invisible passenger sitting next to him.

Yet their car kept moving forward. Soon the four of them would be together as a family for the first time in a year. It was a miracle. Tyray knew he had made it happen as he gazed out the window.

Under the warm Sunday morning sun, the highway stretched out before them, full of twists and uncertainty. But for Tyray, it was grounded in something even stronger.

Hope.

Chapter 1

"Oh my God, Tarah! Check out this picture!" yelled Rochelle Barnes, Tarah Carson's twenty-year-old cousin. Rochelle sat on the rumpled lime green couch in Tarah's living room, leafing through an old photo book.

"Can we stop with the pictures already?" Tarah protested, eyeing the stack of old albums piled on the floor. Her cousin kept flipping the pages as if Tarah hadn't said a word.

"Look at this one!" Rochelle said with a cackle. "Your braids look crazy, girl. And look at all them beads! Remember how we used to wear 'em back in the day?"

"You wore braids too, Aunt Tarah?" asked Kayla, Rochelle's four-year-old daughter. Even though she and Tarah

1

were cousins, Kayla had always called Tarah her aunt.

"That's right, Kayla. I wore 'em just like you," Tarah said, gently resting her hand on the little girl's shoulder. She didn't want Kayla to know that she hated looking at old pictures of herself, especially the ones Rochelle had grabbed.

"Here's another one," Rochelle said, pointing to a photograph. "See how much you and Aunt Tarah look alike, Kayla? You almost look like you could be sisters." The little girl smiled shyly and ate one of the grapes Tarah had given her as a snack.

Rochelle and Kayla lived with Tarah's aunt Lucille in a small stucco house a few blocks away. Nearly every weekend, usually Saturday mornings, Rochelle and Kayla walked over for a visit. Often, Rochelle would leave her daughter there for a few hours so she could get her shopping done. Tarah didn't mind. She loved playing with her little cousin or taking her to the park not far from Bluford High School, where Tarah would start eleventh grade in another month.

Looking at the stack of photo albums next to Rochelle, Tarah wished she could go for a walk right now. Anything

THE BLUFORD SERIES
STORIES TO EXPERIENCE

Visit **www.townsendpress.com**
for a complete list of our books